MW01115446

FOR A WOMAN

DICK SNYDER

authorHOUSE®

AuthorHouse™
1663 Liberty Drive
Bloomington, IN 47403
www.authorhouse.com
Phone: 833-262-8899

© 2022 Dick Snyder. All rights reserved.

No part of this book may be reproduced, stored in a retrieval system, or transmitted by any means without the written permission of the author.

Published by AuthorHouse 10/12/2022

ISBN: 978-1-6655-7351-1 (sc)
ISBN: 978-1-6655-7349-8 (hc)
ISBN: 978-1-6655-7350-4 (e)

Library of Congress Control Number: 2022918979

Print information available on the last page.

Any people depicted in stock imagery provided by Getty Images are models, and such images are being used for illustrative purposes only.
Certain stock imagery © Getty Images.

This book is printed on acid-free paper.

Because of the dynamic nature of the Internet, any web addresses or links contained in this book may have changed since publication and may no longer be valid. The views expressed in this work are solely those of the author and do not necessarily reflect the views of the publisher, and the publisher hereby disclaims any responsibility for them.

This is a work of fiction. All of the characters, names, incidents, organizations, and dialogue in this novel are either the products of the author's imagination or are used fictitiously.

CONTENTS

Acknowledgments...vii

Chapter 1   Bobby Banfield 1
Chapter 2   Family 7
Chapter 3   Goodbuddies................................... 13
Chapter 4   Black on White 19
Chapter 5   Reunion 29
Chapter 6   Night Moods 35
Chapter 7   The Pitch 45
Chapter 8   Hooking Up 55
Chapter 9   Quicksilver..................................... 65
Chapter 10 A New Role 75
Chapter 11 Trey's Gambit 85
Chapter 12 Nibbling.. 91
Chapter 13 Hold The Bucket............................ 97
Chapter 14 A Pause.. 105
Chapter 15 Chaining The Lion........................ 111
Chapter 16 Vegas 119
Chapter 17 She Sings..................................... 127
Chapter 18 Chitlin' Circuit............................ 135
Chapter 19 La Vien Rose 145
Chapter 20 Crossin' Over 151
Chapter 21 Celebration 155

ACKNOWLEDGMENTS

From its first rough edges to the completed narrative, *For A Woman*, has been influenced by the ideas and thoughts of my friend, Ken Sorenson. Our conversations produced ideas and creative imaginings that energized my lethargy and send me back to my iPad. Trey Thaxton's account of his origins, in italics, Chapter Three, is Ken's prose.

Similarly, without the inquiry from Doyce Burke as to whether I might be interested in a family booklet created by her father, Dick Bullard and his brother, Ted, I would have been without a critical element of the narrative. Doyce also offered me some timely suggestions on how to treat Shontel's career, and provided excellent feedback on different drafts.

Rusty Bullard, Perfect Ted's son, and Doyce's cousin, shared stories of the Bullard family, particularly those of his father and "Tricky Dicky". Rusty's flavored reporting, in cadence and candor, informed the story line and gave me multiple touch points to pursue and incorporate into the larger adventure.

I thank also J.D. Blair, in particular, for his candid review of an early effort and accompanying encouragement for another. Paula Yewdall read and commented on a late draft. Norm Stuckey, Jan Stuckey, Maurine Ratekin and James Bockrath provided helpful feedback at various stages of this story.

To view pictures of the various characters, go to: Jonaskirk.com

CHAPTER 1

BOBBY BANFIELD

My uncles were so poor, they needed a ladder to see over a furrow.
Arlo Bullock

Copa, Texas, 1937:

Dick Bullock walked around the circle of chains, paused. Looked down at the drill pipe, noticed a slight vibration. He stopped, checked the rotary and took a quick glimpse of the rig top. He stepped away, felt the tone in the wood permeating the soles of his boots, tickling, then irritating his feet. He knew this feeling; he knew this moment; he knew to run, leaping off the derrick floor, landing in the dirty, sandy earth streaked with tool drippings and clots of oil. He tumbled, rolled, got to his feet, hollering, "She's gonna blow...get the fuck outa' here...get outa' here!" A scatter, as metal hats and tanned faces ran for safety... jumping, scrambling, tumbling ...anything to get off that rig. Thirty seconds after the first warning, the vibration became a roar...growing, accelerating, deepening, finally exploding...splitting ears, blowing pipe, casting chains and tool fragments into a 360 degree race to catch heaving butts and leaden legs. Pressurized liquid tar spewed into the sky and onto the waste surrounding the rig, covering footprints and fractured metal, leaving leaking, stained disarray.

A half-dozen splattered faces and winded bodies touched their life force and found it intact, fit to drill another day. But Dick Bullock cursed the mess and went looking for a new career, one that paid more, cost less, and dressed better. He joined his brother Ted in learning bank robbery from their Uncle Frank, a talent that demanded nerve, timing and stealth, but paid very well indeed. Tricky Dick and Perfect Ted, as they came to be called, survived World War II, and once home, they began a new line of work, opening a Gentleman's Strip Club near Longview, Texas. There they practiced another version of slick slippery and congenial cons, trading the skills of escaping law enforcement for the hard rules of mob life. It was dangerous, as was war, as was drilling oil, as was robbing banks, but it was far more lucrative, and their clothes stayed clean. I wasn't there for their coming of age party, but as with an exploding can of confetti, it spread itself widely, touched the whole Bullock family and brought me a late-in-life renaissance.

My wife, Delta, and I used to talk about the Post-War World, cause it held vivid family memories in her household and in mine. Our own meeting came when we were in Sixth Grade, Copa Elementary, a school serving a small collection of homes west of Longview. When asked about me, she was known to have said, "I don't like his personality". I still kidded her about that every so often, 'cause I liked how I changed her mind a decade later. Course, I doubt I compared well with her dad, Tricky Dick.

He spent a couple of decades working Gentleman's Club venues which were integrated with the mob, then took Delta, her brother Toby, and wife, Ruby, to California. Redding was a flatland of its own, mountains providing both visual relief and shelter from his mischievous years. Tricky took up legitimate living, working and directing construction on dams and bridges, keeping his humor and living a good life. And well before he left Copa, he bought a permanent marker, fencing off 2,000 acres of good land…running cattle on some of it, planting alfalfa, cotton and occasionally carrots on the rest. He called it his Bar Delta Ranch, and it sat between Longview and Lake O' Pines, its frontage extending 800 ft. along the shore. So, as Delta likes to tell it, "We may have been spattered in Texas oil, but we ate a lot of carrots, swam when we wanted and kept our horses fat on alfalfa."

"Redding was different," she said. "No horses, no cattle, no black grime. Drier than Copa too. Went to high school…great experience… nice teachers. Scenery was pretty, but I missed the Bar Delta, not the oil…the water.

Didn't know much at all about my uncles and my aunt, just completely unaware of the hard life, edgy behavior and strings connecting my family to the rest of the Bullocks."

Well, strings connect strangers as well as siblings. A decade after that seventh grade rejection, I met Delta again in Boulder, during our third year at the university. My roommate, Cliff, and I had arranged blind dates with two sisters of AOPi and one of them had brown eyes. Cliff had a rule about not dating a girl who did not have blue eyes, so Delta became my partner for the evening, and as it turned out, for life. For his part, Cliff went on to marry a blue-eyed woman who produced four, blue-eyed children before leaving him in a black and blue divorce. He honed his anger toward Miss Blue Eyes by concealing his coin collection in the property settlement, burying it under her nose in the backyard of her new home where it remained for over a decade. When she sold the house, he quietly dug up his treasure. "She never got a cent," he grins.

By that time, Delta and I had married, and I had met Tricky Dick. I kept my distance from him, in part because we lived far away, and in part because I was never sure if his smile were genuine, warm and welcoming, or calculating, mischievous and edgy. But from time to time, I learned snippets about him, and his brothers. I say, "snippets" because they themselves said little about their activities to the women of the family, protecting them from hearing about what one might call "derring-do" and what others might call robbery.

So, of Tricky Dick's exploits, I knew only what Delta knew, but his decision to buy that haven near Copa, and call it a retreat, became a treasured family gift. It was a world of space, crops, cattle and horses, topics I knew nothing about 'til Delta became ill, and we retired there. We settled right in, and she walked every yard of it trying to maintain her muscle tone and strength as ALS took its toll. Seemed to me there were little picturesque scenes everywhere, and later, I wandered them alone, remembering her bright eyes and courage, soaking up the silence, learning to love its seasons and the cattle who silently wandered about, each meal under their noses. I sold all the horses but Lark, the only one I felt safe riding. Delta and I chose not to have children, and her death left me to reflect on the life I had lived. I judged it to have been responsible, focused, awash with the soft cloth of education, collegiate administration and retirement packages. I didn't see any particular future...just time and decline.

I started arranging and re-arranging my memories, mentally constructing an autobiography which had no particular ending, seemingly fading away each night as might lightly printed ink. My life seemed unexceptional to me, innocent in its structured progression, insulated from the hard lessons of corporate maneuvering, political vengeance, or divorce mayhem. I rode a smooth wave.

Somewhat to my surprise, my professional life had landed me a college presidency at a quality school in the middle of a resonant Twin Cities. Middleton College was well endowed, claimed an alumni scattered across the United States and Europe, and operated on a spacious campus. I never knew much about architecture, but I knew what looked good, and what felt good, and Middleton College did both. When I showed it to my friend, Trey, a few years ago, he described it as *Classic Midwest Traditional*.

One entered campus directly into a brick-walled Main Hall. A satellite low-slung class room building squatted 20 yards to its West. Behind Ol' Main, a few dorms housed fresh faces away from home for the first time. Posted on the edge of the landscape were two contributions from the 1970s, a light-boned, glass walled Science Building and a swarthy, neutered structure for Student Activities. Apart from Main Hall (old) and Science (new) the collection of walls and roofs reminded one of eighth grade projects. Serviceable. Still, within those brick walls of Old Main, life adventures erupted, affecting both the academic postures of the college and those who taught, led and published. It was home, and as in every home, there were stories and there were secrets…some ugly, some redeeming.

Middleton was perfect for me. It had a reputation as one of those "special" experiences anxious parents and desperate students searched to find, and I added to that perception, creating a *School for Theatre and Film which* attracted a national clientele of writers, directors, actors and musicians. In time, I flavored it with summer programs for clowns, startling traditionalists, and we became unique amidst small college cultural attractions. Enrollment grew 10% and we made headlines enough the *Chronicle* rated us among the top five private, small colleges in the nation. Good for us, I figured, and I felt that my work there would be something to remember, for a least a few years.

But to be remembered really meant to be gone, and I had trouble deciding when to leave until Delta became ill. I felt drained…and old. "It's time," I told her. "You're getting weaker. I'm 50 and tired. Let's get outa' here." I negotiated a generous retirement package with the Regents, and we quietly disappeared, settling in Copa, Texas and those 2,000 acres Tricky Dick left his daughter.

Sure, I had some mixed memories of my times at Middleton… conflicts both professional and personal often set me clenching my jaw at night so hard I had to cap three teeth. Watching over academics and their sensitive temperaments took energy, sometimes disdain. Some carried their ambition much as a pot carried boiled eggs. Cook them too hot and they split, flaws spewing a congealed yellow, laced with sloppy white strands of protein gently swirling amidst boiling water. Those, I gently poured away.

But in the months after we took up space at Bar Delta, I decided to write a book about the jabberwocky mismatch of talent and egos at Middleton College, taking care to describe how we tried to educate students amidst gossip, racial tensions, petty jealousy, anger and corrupt sex. It was very good therapy.

I didn't tell the whole story to Delta, but she commented about the tossing I did every so often at night, murmurs about "he deserved it", "give them more teaching hours", "slutty politics" and "her eye popped out". When questioned, all I could say was I was having a bad dream. But I knew when I wrote my book, someone was gonna' die.

Dreams let me ask a different question. What was I going to do in Texas, a land so large with egos so big? How long would Delta live? I had a good retirement and an option to do nothing and think a lot. It felt good. I was young, well youngish. For me, leaving Middleton College was the right thing...and the easiest thing...to do. Settling down in Copa not only brought Delta and me back into our childhood haunts, it gave me opportunity to learn something more about her extended family, and my God, it had an interesting history. Bullocks covered big parts of Texas, flowing later into Colorado, California, Nevada and Arizona, and I began to ask Delta a lot of questions about her uncles (six of them) and her dad, Tricky Dick. She tried to answer me, but usually the talk ended up with something like, "You know, he and Perfect Ted did a lot of things together after the war...before we moved to California..but they just didn't say much." Still curious, I decided to discover more about the Bullock family history.

CHAPTER 2

FAMILY

They did what they had to do, and they did it well.
Arlo Bullock

Delta's closest family contact turned out to be her cousin, Arlo Bullock, Perfect Ted's son, and a cheerful, energetic follower of every lesson his daddy taught him. Arlo was in his 50s, still in the family business, whatever it was, living in Denver. I gave him a call, expecting little, but soon overwhelmed with stories I absorbed as instantly as a teen-age boy might burn images when seeing a towel dropped from a naked woman.

Arlo's voice, clean and clear, led me into every corner of Delta's family. "The first thing you need to know about my dad and Delta's dad is that they were brothers in flesh and spirit, and they were crooks. They robbed banks, worked with the mob, managed a few strip joints and shipped illegal booze for a lot of years."

He paused. Took a breath.

"Well, that's all news to me, Arlo, and to Delta. She says you probably have stories about her Dad she hasn't heard."

"Oh, I'm sure. You know Tricky Dick didn't get that nickname from providing charity to the poor. Every one of those seven Bullock brothers came from poverty so low they had to climb a ladder to see over a furrow. And then their dad died and shortly after so did their mother. They and their sister could have scattered in the wind and dust, 'cause it blew hard and hot in Oklahoma. But they didn't."

"My God...how'd they survive losing both parents...so close together?"

Arlo paused, "Well, an Aunt took in the youngest, three year old Jake, and the rest found their way to Texas, where Uncle Frank and wife, Birdie, ran the *Eat More Café* near the Sabine River. Uncle Frank was a 'businessman', a phrase covering all kinds of activity, some of it legal. But he took 'em under his wing, gave 'em shelter in a shotgun house next to his and taught Tricky Dick and my dad a way to find money inside brick buildings and rickety storefronts."

"Some teacher, eh, that Uncle Frank?"

"Oh yes! But some things Tricky learned for himself. He once sold and removed the swamp cooler off of another guy's house while he was at work, and he peddled a lot of what we called "Midnight Ethyl", draining it out of condensing tanks around oil wells, selling it to guys who liked to sing with their pings. But he was always laughing, even as he sorted through hard times and spare cash. So, yeah, I know things about Tricky, but what I remember most about him was his humor, his intelligence, his smooth talk, and his ability to raise himself from a dust-eatin' orphan into a builder of dams and guardian of good, middle-class wealth."

"A romantic, would you say?"

"Hmmmm...well, maybe. One of his tricks, when robbing a bank, if he saw a teller looking at him with soft eyes...he'd ask her to escort him out of the bank...for his own safety. Then, he'd put a folded $20 bill behind her ear and leave with a smile. Romantic? Yeah...but when he met Delta's mom, Ruby, that put a stop to his lookin'. He loved to tell the story of how she once shot a deer, went to clean it, and it gored her with an antler. Impaled, she dragged the deer into the nearby lake and drowned it. He needed a woman like that...tough and healthy...

she outlived him by half a decade. Yep, Ruby was a survivor…and so was he."

"How about you, Arlo…any special stories about your parents?"

"Oh, yeah…as you would likely suspect, their courtship was unusual. My dad was up on Uncle Frank's roof, fixing a leak in the *Eat More Café,* while Aunt Lilly was down below feeding Bonnie and Clyde. My mom, Ginger, walked by and my dad was so taken with her, stared so hard, he fell off the roof. She didn't look back. Not long after, he saw her in a honky-tonk, her date so drunk my dad had to drive them both home…my mom thanking him for saving her evening. They started dating, and married. I have a couple of sisters."

I listened…took a bit of a breath, "Well, Delta's gonna be surprised to hear her dad robbed banks, but as you say, it was hard times, and she has nothing but good memories, even if they always seemed a little thin. Was Tricky a little like Bonnie and Clyde?"

"Nah! Not at all. First thing to know is that Clyde was gay, and he and Bonnie robbed anything they came across…killed a lot of people just for the sound of guns going off. Took a long time to catch 'em and even then that Sheriff Hamer had to break the law and cross county lines to shoot 'em up in an ambush. I know they sound romantic, Bonnie and Clyde, but the closest any of us came to their doin's was when our Uncle Frank fed 'em and sold 'em supplies out of the back door of his store, down near the Sabine. They'd buy goods, camp down by the water and then head out to rob some more. Everyone's heard of Bonnie and Clyde. No one's heard of my Uncle Frank and that's the way he liked it."

"About yourself. I hear you took over the business from your dad, 'Perfect Ted'. Is that really what the family called him?"

"Oh, yeah. He just tried to do anything he took up as well as he could."

"Was there a 'Bobby James' in the family? Or a 'Jim Bob'?" I was joking a bit, but Arlo did me one better.

"Well, no, but we had 'Chuck-a-Luck' and 'Bullet Ben'."

I gave in. "Did that seem odd...all these nicknames?"

"Nah. I know it sounds a little bizarre, but that's just kind of an Oklahoma/Texas habit. Christian name and family name...nothing legal, but a real moniker in family lore. Wasn't a rule to give 'em out, but Jake's the only one of my uncles who doesn't have a name different from the one on the birth certificate."

"And yours is just plain 'Arlo', eh?"

"Yep. New generation."

I moved on. "So, Arlo, Rule One was be a crook. How'd that work out?"

"Well, better than I might have thought. Even dad seemed a little puzzled that he could maneuver through the world of hard business, what I call "knickers-crime"...you know all that stuff surrounding strippers, booze, gambling and a little prostitution...and not get caught. But he was one of the first to sell liquor by the drink, a near novelty that kept men in the bar spending money. And in those days, they didn't have liquor licenses, inspectors, or law enforcement to worry about...not really. A little money bought a lot of understanding. And remember, the counties were close together, and a sheriff in one county had no jurisdiction in another. Rob a bank in one...live easily 20 miles away. Texas Rangers were out there somewhere I guess, but he never saw 'em."

"Lot of life lessons to be taught in that business, eh?"

"You bet. One of my dad's most lasting insights was that he would rather deal with the mob than with politicians...and he had connections going all the way to Frank Sinatra, who helped him put professional entertainers in his clubs, to Joe Civello, the number two guy in the Marcello family before Dom Ri'chard moved up. In Dallas, Civello was closely connected to Jack Ruby."

"And Kennedy?"

"There's a story there…"

"Ummph…well apart from being a successful crook, any other family rules?"

"Well, Rule Two was don't tell the women anything. I know all the stories, where the businesses grew up, how we connected to the mob and why we succeeded…when I say 'we', I'm talkin' family, you know, but especially my dad, cause Tricky Dick pretty much left the business during Vietnam.

The mob…again. But then, what was I expecting? I had clearly stumbled into a jackpot of family information, and Delta was gonna feel a little exposed by all of it, but I'd remind her of the hard times her mother told her about, and the desperation they often had to put food on the table. Her dad, Tricky Dick, just did what he had to do.

"That shotgun house you mention, Arlo. What's that…a weapons depot?"

He laughed, "Nope, it's a bare-bones building with each room adjoining the other…no hallway…all the way to the back where the kitchen emptied its heat into the air. No indoor plumbing…each room, 12' wide usually, had a door opening to the next room. It's a long, narrow structure, much like the barrel of a shotgun. Originally a slave structure, it was just what the Bullock's needed..space enough to grow up and find a future, and they all did."

'Lots a' stories about the kids and choices, eh?"

"More than I have time to tell right now, but you just stay in touch, and I'll spit 'em out as they come to me…they make a good tale and something to laugh about at Sunday supper."

And that's the way it started. A pretty straight-shooting, small town boy who became a college President, retiring to his wife's birthright home in Texas, watching her die, wondering what to do in the emptiness. I lived a new life now, quietly unscheduled, far from controversy, tuned by wispy, sifting breezes and the scent of cow manure and cut alfalfa. While I was mulling a book about disappointed, angry faculty, Arlo kept giving me family stories, turning fables upside down and leaving me sifting reality. Though I could not see it at the time, his storytelling and my lingering dislike of obnoxious faculty led to the best thing I accomplished after Delta died. And I'll tell more about that in a bit.

CHAPTER 3

GOODBUDDIES

I split his head just above the hairline of
his beautiful blond pompadour.
Trey Thaxton

Treyson Thaxton showed up about the time I turned 13, both of us wondering what life would be all about. We entered Copa High together, strangers in a maze of hallways, clattering lockers and the buzz of soft gossip. He was tall, of Norwegian heritage, and a bit of a looker in the midst of plain faces. He had moved into Copa without a sound, the family just appearing in the Big Bag Grocery, shopping... and they didn't go away.

I first caught sight of him walking to school one morning early in our Freshman year. I always tried to pass by a drive-in where evening consumers of cherry cokes and hamburgers might drop a little change in their haste to go parking on dark roads among the oil wells. I found an occasional dime, sometimes a quarter, more often a few pennies.

This day I had a companion, a stranger in my usual lineup of well-worn faces, walking about appearing as confused and puzzled about life as I myself was. He was searchin' for change too, and we exchanged glances, greetings and bonded...an attraction between two of the same ilk.

I was curious about him not just from this silent sharing of the nickel and dime game, but because he looked so different. Copa, Texas was the land of cross border Cajuns from Louisiana, migrating Germans from Indiana and wandering Oakies. There were no Norwegians, and I had to ask, "What brought you here? How long you staying?" He evaded my inquiries, but I respected that. Everyone had stories about themselves they didn't want to tell.

We became friends, not knowing it was for life, just feeling that it would get us through a week of learning about high school, padlocked lockers and strange looks from new people. We took up wandering the halls together because, at the time, neither one of us could brave public scrutiny alone, and walking alongside a girl just invited grief, both from her and the watchers hanging on the walls of the corridors.

We were different from one another, Trey and I. Sports were my passion, family my strength. He didn't play any games 'til he was all grown and found out how well he could strike a golf ball. Back in the day, he kept his thoughts about his family, its anger and his estrangement buried in small expletives, mumbles and little swear words with no particular direction. Sometimes a comment, a complaint, might leave me curious and a little frightened for him. But the whole story was a long time coming.

I described my home life with single words: quiet; loving; challenging; poor. But ignorance of Trey's family kept my imagination active, conjuring images that cramped my gut, creating scenarios that could tell me something about my friend he didn't want to share. Silence is like that. What we can't see, we can invent, but I wasn't having much luck explaining what I saw in front of me. What made Trey tick?

It took some time, but on one of our semi-sober evenings, riding a wave of booze, I asked Trey straight on what his life had been about... what he thought about his family. His answer nearly paralyzed me, 'cause it was pretty much on the other side of the world from mine. But this is what he said.

We lived in Bomar, Oklahoma from 1937 'til 1949. My dad had come from the East, a wild, runaway, full blooded Norwegian, workin' for the CCC. Knocked up my ma'am, an Okie Cree woman. I was born smart and sleek. She held me in high adoration. Pa didn't like that, and he didn't like me. Though just a babe in arms, I remember. I didn't like him either.

We grew that way, me hiding mostly when he was around. Then when I was eight or nine, he took to the drink bad. Now, not just mean, but drunk mean.

Bomar had a little shanty of a building that was the Ardmore County Library. I'd go from school to the library. I started at one corner, and read every book on the shelves. There weren't many, mostly paper, but I read them all, some classics, even some Shakespeare.

The library closed at seven, so I'd head home. He'd usually been drunken out by then. She'd bring them both to bed, after putting a couple sticks in the stove and leave' me something in the oven.

That night, when I came in, he was bent over her on the floor, blood under her head. He was weepy and shouting, "I didn't mean to". I watched to see her breathe. She didn't.

There was a large cast iron skillet on the stovetop, half filled with lard. When I picked it up, he turned his bleary eyes on me. I swung the pan...gave it everything. His head split just above the hairline of his beautiful blond pompadour, revealing red and gray.

The law said "justified", and sent me here to Copa to live with Ma's sister, Joey. Nobody but them knows this story, Bobby, and Injuns don't talk.

I knew stories about the contrast between Paul McCartney's home life and John Lennon's...Ying and Yang. But theirs was a love spat compared to the difference between what I lived and what Trey had to endure. I thought of those rock icons even as I listened to him, absorbing the alienation, the violence, the anger that welled up in his voice when he explained his family. His stories were crackling spits of flame compared to the calm waters upon which my family floated its raft.

But that was Trey's story, and he was stickin' to it, and I wasn't telling anyone about it, least not til' now. And not long after he told me, we found ourselves in a different fight, not with parents, but with a couple of older teen-agers who thought it was fun to drive along the hills and play bumper cars. Now, you may wonder what that was all about, but it was just this. Pull your car up behind another, parked with lights out, and maybe a boy and girl inside. Push the gas down a bit and give them a bump that might well be out of sync with the ones they were making inside the car. Panic! Clothes flying! Lots of laughter from the Bumpers.

Well, we had done that a couple of times..have to admit it...and it was fun all right, but this one night, we were just sitting there sipping Brew 102, and we got bumped, and we weren't liking it. Out of the car we jumped, me planning on mouthing loud insults, but Trey, being Trey I guess, he just walked right to the car behind us, reached in the open window, grabbed the driver as he opened the car door and started hitting him in the face.

I was astounded! Out the other door jumped the friend, planning on grabbing and bashing Trey, and no sooner had he crossed the hood, I shouted, just like in the movies I thought later, "Look out Trey... comin' behind ya", and took leave of my senses. I took a reflexive leap, and jumped his back...hitting him in the face as he twirled about trying to throw me off.

I was too scared to let go, and kept swinging, battering his face while Trey had the other guy on the ground, putting his fists all over him. When my guy just ran for the dark, I dropped off and grabbed

Trey's arms, pinned them to his side, and shouted, "He's all done, Trey…let him go!"

He did and the guy just lay there. We caught our breath for a few minutes, looked around into the dark, finding nothing, walked back to our car, drove to a small alleyway on the edge of Copa and finished our brews. We didn't say much, but the bonds were signed, in fists and blood.

A week later, Trey handed me a half-dozen pencil drawings showing scenes from Bumper Night. Only a few lines in each but they were dramatic portraits of dark, violent release. I didn't know if his drawings were good art, but they caught my attention, and I understood more clearly what made him tick, and it wasn't the internal clock of human kindness. We made it through high school that way, sampling the dating game, evading the marriage trap…sex was sort of a hands-on thing. We thought we were lovers waiting for the right woman to show up, and our future was nothing to worry about.

Until it was.

Trey took up an entry level, local job in drafting. It wasn't art, but his skills translated well into making precise lines, and he had a rare intelligence in being able to envision what it might take to loop pipes and wires or build anything from a two-room Tiny House to a four story business center, and he had hopes, he later told me, of getting into the home-design business. Well, he had an idea about his future. I didn't have a single one.

I continued living like a high-schooler attending the Junior College in Longview. It was, for me, a brave step out of the flow of most of my friends who turned a high school degree into small town marriages and children. For a couple of years, it seemed to work nicely. I worked part time, fumbling through classes, missing a few pals who graduated and moved on to colleges. Couldn't see myself doing that.

What I wanted...all I wanted...was a full time girlfriend who would keep me in her dreams and pin my body to her seams. But when I looked around, none of the pretty faces I courted seemed to be as needy or as lonely as I. And keen as I was about girls, I had no idea what sex was about...not really...fumbling around and mini-ejaculations didn't count. Were those bumbles the essence of courtship? I was a White boy with tightly held values of propriety, repressed sexuality, and a wish that the perfect girl would find me. I stayed that way until I met Shontel.

CHAPTER 4

BLACK ON WHITE

Honey, no one puts a hand on me, 'less I want them to.
Shontel

Somewhere in my first two years of junior college and Trey's migration from draftsman to local citizen, we both took up with Shontel Williams, a Black senior and honor student at Rosa Parks High. I don't quite remember how either one of us got started with Shontel...maybe it was a summer dance...but I do remember her being the subject of intense conversation throughout my time in junior college, cause first she was dating Trey, then me, then Trey again, and who knows who lay between her legs in between. Neither of us really cared. We just kept our eyes on her, waiting for our turn on the Merry-Go-Round.

And, thinking back, I guess if I had to choose a girl to have had my first real sex with, it would have been Shontel. She knew things. She was confident. She nurtured an amateur's insecurity, free in her spirit, ruthless in her right to choose. She changed a lot of things in my life, Shontel did, and some of them stained permanently. Shontel...a single word and a multi-colored life. She could tenderize a tough guy, harden a coward or shame a blowhard. She was...and she remained... the answer for every question I had about living well and loving deeply. She wasn't a permanent resource, but she was an encyclopedia of knowledge, and when she finished creating one phase of me or the other, she left me on my own. But for a year or two, I went to school with her, in and out of bed.

I'd ask her sometimes how she came to be so easy with sex, and she would just smile at me...real big...and say, "My mama told me there's things about life you don't want to miss, and they come in different packages...sample them all." Well, as I learned that year, and in the years to come, she didn't miss much. I heard all about how some girls were exploited in their homes by cousins, uncles, even brothers, but when I would brush up to these ideas with Shontel, she would just look me in the eye, "Ain't nobody touching this body without me sayin' so."

I felt good about that cause I was touching it a lot. But then, my turn ended, and she took up with Trey in between a couple of other boyfriends. Back and forth...maybe a better expression is "round and round" but whatever the axis, she lived life without listening to commands and without restraint, and she demanded respect by the very way she carried herself. Shontel. She's gonna go somewhere with that personal pride, we thought. She's got grit. On that both Trey and I agreed.

She loved to talk, sometimes nonstop, and in her machine-gun speed of telling, I heard about her life before Copa. Her father, Elijah Williams, came from the cotton fields but left Georgia for Louisiana, thinking harvesting sugar cane, might be better for them, maybe less racist, maybe better for his family of six, those five boys and Shontel. It was different all right... harder, back-breaking...and it was difficult to say which placed a larger imprint on the family, being Black, being descended from slaves or being sliced by chopping cane. Elijah was born free, true enough, but the vestiges of Black bondage affected him just as it affected every Black face I've ever known. Shontel's mother, Calista, made money practicing New Orleans voodoo, paying no difference to various cultural strains of the dark art coming in from Cuba and Haiti, preferring to describe herself as Madam Unique and daring anyone to challenge it.

She set up shop in a small, old blacksmith frame building, known locally as the Jean Lafitte Home. Locals kept it from falling apart in honor of Lafitte's privateer assault against the British back in the day...way back. The shop reeked with both the history of the War of 1812 and a touch of wood rot, New Orleans being humid and sometimes swamped with week-to week Caribbean storms. It was all fine for Calista. She practiced her arts at midnight, lying to losers who wanted to understand past failures and envision future successes. In daytime, she built influence in her community by reporting the fictions of the night.

For nearly five years, Elijah and Calista found their way, making a life free of slavery, one encapsulated into the racist but understood ways of Louisiana and the South in general. But, there came a time when Depression took everyone down, kept fortune seekers and tellers looking through empty coin sacks and sent Blacks by the tens of thousands heading north, Detroit way.

Elijah thought differently, persuading Calista to leave her dark magic and moving the family to Shreveport where there was talk of work in the oil fields. They spent a few months there, lingering, and finally made a final move across the border to a small town on the edge of Longview, Texas. Elijah sometimes passed as White, found work... and kept it. Calista took caution as her guide for several months, then quietly began telling fortunes and advising edgy customers on mystical arts and the future of their love lives. Of that advice, love... and sex...she had much to offer paying marks, but she shared her wisdom with Shontel free of charge.

Without incident, they finally settled into Copa, Shontel being 10 years old when they arrived, 15 when she hit Rosa Parks High School theatre program. Within a year, she was a local legend where her ability to sing, dance, and act changed her from a large-eyed little girl, into a wise teen-woman who lived years ahead of her classmates. She kept her hair short, body tight and her smile under control. Rosa Parks High had no competitors for her talented ambition, and her performances transformed audiences, blending Blacks and Whites into a light brown mosaic.

Something about Shontel's Creole origins, her mama's belief in Voodoo and its rituals startled me. I noted the freedom it gave her to live a life unfettered by Christian precepts, spinning instead the realities of on-the-street living. She wore needles in her hair when she grew it out, kept matches, incense and a Derringer in her purse. But I was uneasy with the dark arts, suspicious of the guidance her mother gave her, and cautious about falling into some kind of witchery abyss. Shy, still uneducated to the rituals of the bed, I saw Shontel as a bit of cotton candy...sweet, alluring, tasty, disappearing on the tip of the tongue. But over time, she took on a more substantive flavor in my life...and changed it.

She was tall, nearly 6 feet, slender, with large hands, quick feet and a figure she herself described as "Dorothy Dandridge Perfect". She had a generous mouth, perfectly balanced lips and reams of hair seemingly bewitched with its ability to adapt to style, events and mood. She could wrap it, braid it, flare it or bunch it, and it always looked good...as did she. For protection she placed steel pins in her locks, to go with the Derringer in her purse. Look at her wrong or mouth an insult, and out came a needle, or her fists, or sometimes the Derringer. She tolerated no conversation which used the word, "Nigger". That could get you killed.

She was full of sayings dredged from her impressions of what she called the Black Renaissance. "It started in the Twenties," she liked to say, "and every decade since, we been shaking the heavens with passion, fashion and the notes of jazz...piano, horns and smooth lovin'. Harlem is its home and its changing every month...music, art, politics. You White boys gonna have to come find me when I make it to New York."

She likened her voice to that of Etta James, moved with conviction and groomed herself as might Dandridge or Diana Ross. In the hours she wasn't rehearsing, performing, or auditioning, she sank into the black pit of the exhausted, refueling for another day of prep, and another, and another. High school wasn't for passing time. It was time passing over her commitment, taking her closer to the escape and the stardom she hungered for.

"Ain't no White Way gonna keep this girl off the stage," she liked to say...and she said it often.

How you think you're gonna do that, Shontel," we would ask, "Dance your way up to Times Square?"

"It'll all work out, you mutha's, but look out...we all comin' for you White boys," she would joke with Trey and me. Then in a more serious tone, she might mutter, "Maybe, I'm gonna' just save your pale skins for my future." We thought that was some kind of a promise.

We wondered what she told the White woman she left us for. Or the Black man she met in Longview. Soon enough, all three were off to New York to make a career or break their bankroll, or find another part of their swing thing. Shontel was wild, too much for either Trey or myself, but for those moments when we fit her hunger and her tone, we gave our all, and pined to give more. We just couldn't believe it wasn't love.

In New York, Shontel sorted through partners as in a play, keeping her sense of timing and honing her skills as an actress. She could sing with range and nuance...compelling, some thought...and certainly good enough to find weekly work in small clubs, and she could mirror dance with a featured performer. But acting was her passion. On stage, she surrendered herself to every scene, her tone and mood vibrating through her body, perfectly timed to feed the hunger of the audience. Her words, expressions, love looks or violent explosions, all rocketed into the highest seats...and lodged in the heart. She could be scary, loving, or full of loss. Call for it and Shontel could deliver...and New York noticed.

She lived with strangers, found herself traveling enough to amass miles she traded for small, fashionable goods she could parade in public. Happy enough to take out those steel lances in her hair, lay them in an X, and stare down any security screener who looked at them twice. She once told me those pins were dipped in poison. I had no reason not to believe her. She smoked pot with friends, liked her tats, tried and quickly gave up cocaine, took auditions without pause and jumped into bed, or up against a wall, with whomever caught her fancy. Her style of loving, so unedited, so impulsive, so widely shared was probably why Trey and I found it so attractive. And in both the first year I met her and these most recent ones, she remains the most unique figure I have known.

I think both Trey and I each believed we would eventually star in her life movie. She could calm us with a look and a whisper...incite us with a touch and a stroke. But with the quick-time compression that a film could create, the moment we thought either of us were heading into her future, she put us off with rejection or a new partner. And when she suddenly left town, pursuing her dreams, proving to both of us she was a volatile, free spirit, we knew we had no part in what she believed her life would be about. Never did.

More to the point, I thought neither Trey nor I would ever see her again. Her leaving may have been seen as some kind of betrayal, but she gave us plenty of warning, if we wanted to hear it. As she said to both of us from time to time, in and out of bed, "You White boys are fun...just don't go gettin' serious on me, now." I didn't know about love, but Trey believed he had found it with Shontel, and she would remind us every time either one of us started mushing about life with her. "This ain't love, honey. It's just good sex."

But she wasn't waiting around to see what we liked or what we wanted. Her ambition kept her educated both to the whimsy of the moment and the wisdom of the ages. Her degree was in show business, cutthroat talent competitions, skilled performances and an endless supply of stamina. Once in New York, she spent as much time in acting studios and auditions as she did singing a shift in a Harlem bar. She electrified those who saw her perform, banging away at the doors of casting auditions until she began to be cast. They may not have been starring rolls, but she was up on Broadway, and she wasn't coming down. She may have flirted with the excitement of a Harlem renewal, but her eye was always on Shontel...and she solved the maze. Go girl.

When I think back about those days...and I have pondered them a lot lately, I find it hard to explain my infatuation, or was it love, with Shontel. I couldn't really speak her language, nor did I have her intimate understanding of human behavior. I could not dance her music, much less embrace what she called "Black rhythm and blues". But, she liked to talk...and I liked to listen...and for reasons of her own...which would explain everything she did...for reasons of her own...she took to me...probably for my innocence. She was the first girl/woman to take me to bed, to show me her body, to embrace and love mine and give me a confidence and energy that I carried with me the rest of my life.

There was an important lesson in all of this too. I thought sex was a reflection of commitment, an emotional seal that led to an open future. She brought me up short when I tried to explain my thoughts, simply saying, "Sex is for sex, Bobby Banfield. I don't share it lightly, but I don't mistake it for a set of handcuffs either. Just relax and enjoy our time, White boy." She said that last part with a smile and a kiss, and I decided to agree with everything she said.

She told the same thing to Trey, my friend. We didn't share details, but we shared perceptions of Shontel all through the time I was in junior college and he was beginning his career as a draftsman. Then, without any particular plan, Shontel moved on from us and not much later, I moved on from Copa.

I made it through college, one small step at a time, wondering where it would lead, and Trey found a hunger and confidence in himself that led to his private study of construct and design, materials and soils...I likened it to pursuit of a PhD...and a state examination proclaimed him an architect. I thought Shontel would like him best once he made himself into a professional, but she had begun to find night lights and marquees with her name on them. Nothing about Copa, Trey or myself was going to match that. We stayed in touch, especially after the arrival of email, and she remained an occasional correspondent. But we believed she had finally slipped away when she won a Tony for "*The Milkmaid*" and then a Golden Globe nomination for "*Away My Love*".

I don't actually remember ever saying goodbye to Trey. Just, "See you later," but he remained my kind of guy, however distant we lived from one another. I had occasional chats with him, enough to know he was a very successful architect, builder and investor. But St. Paul and Santa Fe were far targets to one another. Delta liked him...wondered why he hadn't married...and I usually just said, "He's waiting on Shontel." I thought I was kidding. Maybe not.

It took an institutional event, a Class Reunion, to put us face to face with the drama that changed our lives. Having lost Delta, I urged Trey to come in a day early for some catching up on life. We spent that first night drinking, sharing stories, some true, and eventually coming back to the subject we could never quite dismiss, Shontel. Somewhere in the stir of the evening and the wavering memories of what we thought we could report, I gave Trey a copy of my latest, "retirement writing". It was a novella, WHY SHE WEPT, an effort to capture the crazy-ass dynamics of a small college and an angry Dean abusing faculty, three of whom, well maybe four, killed her.

For me, it was an exercise in therapy. I could control the characters in ways I never controlled their real-life images. I could reveal all the imaginings I had about what should happen to those who bedeviled me or who attracted me. It was largely a fantasy piece of writing, and I didn't think much of it, handing it over to Trey with an inscription that said, *"Life ain't hard, but it is messy."* But, like many things I let slip by, Trey took the book as an assignment, and by the next morning, the day of the 35th Copa High School Class Reunion, he had an idea that turned our lives, and Shontel's, inside out.

CHAPTER 5

REUNION

Who's gonna show. Who's gonna go? You never know.
Bobby Banfield

As was his habit, Trey was awake when first light touched the tops of the trees. I preferred mid-morning, and when I came down to wipe some of the kitchen floor with my socks, Trey was lost in the book. He had a cup of coffee within an arm's reach, but his eyes were sweeping across pages, one at a time, burying them in his mind..and as it turned out…in his imagination.

I began blending flour, eggs, milk and baking powder, asking whether he wanted his pancakes thin or thick.

"Thin, 'bout six of 'em."

"Honey or syrup?"

"Honey."

"What you findin' so interesting in there?"

"Just followin' along and findin' this character, Dean Sara Stone, a bit weird."

"Well, she was."

"You ever know anyone in real life like her?"

"Well, not quite like her, but close enough."

"She has an edge to her…promises a lot more violence than you show."

"Really. I never thought of her as violent…just voracious."

"Hmmm," Trey took another sip of his coffee.

I started the links in the skillet, waited a few minutes and poured some cakes…watched the bubbles rise…turned them…rolled the sausage and let both pans do their work. Brought out the honey, warmed it to flowing, and retrieved some butter, cool but pliable. Trey kept reading, his ideas maybe forming as did the bubbles on the pancakes, murmuring a bit, but keeping his eyes on the book, not the skillet.

I finally shoveled out the cakes, links too, and set them down, forcing Trey to put the book to the side. He hesitated a bit, then ate, real quick, and got back to his reading, still sippin' coffee. I expected more comment 'bout the book…after all, I wrote it, and I gave it to him, and he was damn near done with it, and all he could say was Sara Stone sounds like a repressed serial killer. Well, I knew that he didn't usually say much 'less he had somethin' in particular to offer, so I waited.

He motioned to his coffee cup. I refilled it. His eyes wandered to the stove, and I browned up a couple more cakes. He ate, but his mind wasn't on food. I recognized the silence and kept my own.

He looked up, wiped his lips and spoke in that low roar of a voice of his. "I been thinking about this book of yours from chapter one…you may have produced some kind of special story here, Bobby, something that just triggers images in my head…and images convert to film and that tells me you and I should make a movie about your book."

I just looked at him…nearly five seconds. "Movie? What the hell is there in there that makes you think it would make a movie, Trey… it's just a story about a trans-gender, crippled, belligerent, bi-sexual Dean who likes to screw in strange places. What about that could you show on a screen?"

"Nah, I'm not thinking 'bout soft-core porn, but I am thinking that when a valued member of a university gets murdered by three different people, maybe four, it could make a film worth watching."

"Trey. I wrote this book. Almost nothing in it suggests a story that would hold an movie audience. It's just university politics and personal frailty...flavored with a little mystery...maybe a little envy, maybe a hint of revenge, but it's mostly just about human weakness, sex and academic politics."

"Oh," he said, "I'm not saying we won't have to change the story a bit."

"Change it?"

"Yep. Gonna need to turn this Sallie Drake from an incompetent into someone evil...dangerous...heartless...cold...useless, someone who terrorizes the university even as she is screwing staff and students to her heart's content. That what makes a movie. A social misfit, without conscience, capable of abandonment, maybe even murder, terrorizing people secure in their places. Need a compelling lead actress who can convince us she is a violent, sexual predator. That calls for a tight screenplay, a haunting, edgy musical score and a great director who can inspire his actors. Put a taut story into the hands of a skilled professional and there's no telling where it will end.

"Really?"

"Remember *'Leave Her To Heaven?'* It was a vicious film about a jealous wife who murdered a handicapped boy just to keep her husband to herself. But the vision of her abandoning the youngster in the middle of a lake haunted moviegoers for a year. Led to an Academy Award nomination for Jean Tierney and a terrible memory for me to carry. Nobody forgets stuff like that. So, if the story is taut and the actors know what they're doing, there's a chance to thrill an audience and pocket big bucks."

I just looked at him.

"Got some more cakes? Another sausage?"

I said nothing. Got up, warmed the skillet, brought out a few more links and stirred the batter...good to go. A few minutes and into their pans they went, sort of like Trey and me right now...interested in being fed entertainment, but cooking it up in different formats... mine was a book and it was in print. His was a movie and it was gonna take a lot more cookin'.

"Trey, I don't know what you got hidden away, but my money is structured in retirement funds and land. My big plan for the next two years is to build a house somewhere on the property, somewhere near the lake where evening breezes search it out. I got no cash for adventures...and movies cost money...lots of money. Where we gonna find something like that...who invests in movies, huh?"

"You say you're building a house...a new home right here on the property?"

"Well, yeah. There's lots of reminders about Delta still here and I'm all right with that, but I want something a little smaller...a little more intimate...I guess its a part of moving on."

"You asking me to build your new home?"

Silence, and my mind spun in three different directions. Hadn't thought of hiring Trey as a builder. My budget too small? What was he doing that he had time? An overture to hang around? Maybe.

"You asking me to hire you to do it?"

"Why not? I got nothing doing these days. My CEO runs things, and he doesn't need me to clutter up his planning. Truth to tell I'm a little weary of spending time in Santa Fe, and tired of selling design to the pseudo-Indians in the desert and those California bleached-teeth, tan faces preoccupied with beaches, traffic and waves. Yeah, I could be interested in fixin' you up in a nice set of comfort and views. You really serious about building?"

"Well, yeah...sure I am...but I didn't plan on doing anything about it for awhile...need to get my financing in place, but I should probably do something about moving ahead with it. You really interested?"

"I am. Don't need to decide just now, but let's keep mulling it over. I'll plan on staying a couple days after the reunion and we'll see if we can find the money."

"Money for the home-build, not the movie. Right."

"Well, yeah, but I don't want to give up on the movie. Just a little longer search...I could find a couple of million I think, but we're gonna need 40-60 times that to make a film and distribute it. We got time."

"That's more money than I would have earned in 20 lifetimes, Trey. Where in the hell could we ever find bucks like that. Eh?"

"Hmmm," he paused. "There is a guy in Dallas I did some work for several years ago...big construction projects...and I always believed he had to be connected somewhere. Guy named Gino Marcello. Well, let's keep that in the back of our minds. You rummage a bit and see what we can dream up. You still in touch with that cousin of Delta's... Arlo? You joked a bit about his having connections to some of the mob money that his dad and Delta's dad tapped into? Weren't you telling me they had a wispy-washy relationship with the law...back in the day. Maybe Arlo knows something about draining dollars out of the darker side of business? Maybe? You think?"

"That's a past I'm not sure I want to be reviving, Trey. But Arlo's full of information and he's been in the business long enough to know what he's doing. Let's grind on this movie idea a bit, and if we stay serious, I'll ring him up and see what he can tell us. Meantime, we have a reunion to go to tonight, and I'm gonna clean the kitchen, take a walk and get a nap. Don't wanna' have to leave the fun early."

"Whose gonna be there...any idea?"

"Nah, I think they invite a couple of classes on each side of ours just to get enough people. These days, I probably couldn't recognize a girl from high school without a name tag. But after a bit of time, personalities fall into place. I've been to two or three of these over the years. Had fun. Delta enjoyed them a lot.

The thought occurred to the two of us at the same time, and we blended our voices: *"Wonder if Shontel's gonna show up?"* Sometimes those Rosa Parks High School girls came to our reunions just to show us how to dance, and when Shontel was with them, everyone pushed the boundaries of propriety. Nice way to say, "Everyone got laid". Yeah, wonder if Shontel would be there.

CHAPTER 6

NIGHT MOODS

I heard his shoulder pop, but Shontel kept
Trey from kicking in his skull.
Bobby Banfield

The flock flees, disappears, returns. There must be something in the world of high school fibs and frolics that accounts for the migrations of graduates into the unseen long enough to describe the journey when they return. Seldom does one hear of a favorite person losing their way. They might choose not to return, but they all know the way. The heart knows.

So it was with Trey and I, dressing carefully with slacks, open throat collared shirt, and well-worn Adidas. Two bachelors unashamed, we loosed ourselves to sample memories, hear new fictions and ogle faces, some still carrying traces of youth. Invigorated with our conversations about books, movies and buildings, we ambled out of the house and headed toward the high school, an amiable distance for early October. Caught the scent of cut alfalfa, a breeze of comfort and the satisfaction we both took from looking Copa over once again. It felt good to amble along in the nicer parts of the little town, avoiding blocks of aged homes, crumbling masonry and the ever-present litter that suggested someone had been out late, drunk and angry…or homeless.

"How comes you never married?"

"How comes you did?"

"Well, it just seemed natural to me to finish college and marry... raise a family. That's what I thought all people did...and most everyone here in Copa followed the pattern. I thought it was a step by step method: college, marriage, children, grandchildren, old age and death."

"You bailed on the children idea, eh?"

"Yep. Delta wasn't keen on having any, and I enjoyed our peace and quiet.

"Nothin' remarkable about that," Trey muttered, "Ain't none of us getting out of here alive. Might as well build it the way you want to live it." He paused, then finished up with, "Didn't you think of wanting more than the ordinary?"

"Oh, for me, it *was* more. You think I could see myself as President of Middleton College while we were walking across the Copa High graduation stage. Hell, I barely knew if I had a job for the summer. I really just stumbled into a career. Filled a lot of emotional baggage doing it, for sure, but well, when Shontel left, my imagination could not replace her. And I sure wasn't gonna go to New York to try and chase her down."

"So where did you meet Delta?"

"Well, in Seventh Grade," I smiled, "At the time, she said she didn't like my personality...you know...kids. Years later, in college, I met her again on a blind date. Not sure I fell in love on the spot, but I was thinking maybe she liked my chatter a bit more this time. I never dated another woman after that night."

"Yeah, that sounds about like you. Just ridin' the rails and pickin' up cargo along the way...long hauler."

"Again, Mister Smooth, how did you escape the marriage setting... single for years, good income in architectural design, edgy patter and witty remarks...who could resist?"

36

"Not many," Trey smiled, "But there was something holding me back...just didn't see myself recreating a family anything like what I grew up in, and a little fearful that I might. Couple of times, I almost settled in with a woman but then the doubt would surface, and the work would erupt and before I knew it, she'd left me for a man who could make a commitment. There was one other thing too."

"Eh? One other thing? What...are you sterile...what?"

"Sterile? Nah, not anything like that. It's just there was always this thing about you know, about Shontel."

Silence.

I looked at Trey from the side. Took a breath and blew out easy. "You fucker. You telling me you're still infatuated with a high school romance that was so potent you rejected every woman you met in life?"

"Well, I didn't reject them...I just didn't marry 'em."

We walked along another two blocks, saw the high school two more to the right and turned. I mussed about a bit, thinking over Trey's thoughts. Shontel. I remembered her as though she were the best dream I ever had, but she just didn't have any place in my daylight. She was special. I wrote her an occasional email in the 90s and after, but it was all just chit-chat. I could have followed her career by reading a Hollywood brag-rag, but I didn't. She was special to me in the way a first love is special, and then it begins to fade in the reality of more enduring memories, in the harsh grinding of life being lived and the trade of imaginative hideaways for daily work. Shontel. Never forgot her. Never thought of her. Just Shontel.

Guess Trey had had his say about marriage. I could see it though I could not have grasped it. I needed something solid to lean against when facing the storms. Delta was all that and more. Intimate in our private moments, cheerful and buoyant amidst strangers, she loved a joke and laughed loud and long when something really tickled her. We didn't feel the desire for children, and she had plenty of family.

From what she told me about her father, Tricky Dick, she had his sense of humor and a way of engaging you in conversation as though you were the only person in a room full of moon faces. I lightly embraced her memory once again, my mind conjuring her image, her laughter and her eyes, beautifully brown in a way that my old roommate, Cliff would never know.

I laughed out loud, Trey glancing at me, wondering what the tickler was, but I was remembering the rest of Cliff's story. His wife with the blue eyes exploded far more often than he could live with, and the divorce wasn't pretty.

I chose brown eyes and they were resilient, loving, flashing on occasion, and we rode life's pony together right up to the end. ALS. Letters meaning "lethal, irrevocable, gutting", and it was all that. Losing Delta so soon after my retirement left me empty, restlessly looking for something on 2,000 acres that could refresh me. So far, no luck. But Trey was here tickling my mind, invigorating my sense of the future, and now, maybe, we could recreate our high school humor at a reunion.

We walked. We ambled. We strolled. In the back of our minds, we wondered if Shontel could possibly show up, as kids from Rosa Parks High sometimes did, embarrassing us with their fluidity, swift chatter and the Black slang that sometimes sounded guttural and sometimes translated into a hip, short version of a word that no longer needed all those letters: "Axed me, foo? S'up? Da't yo' bling? Lay-low J-lo." I mouthed them again as we walked. Weird...but useful. Shontel had taken both Trey and I out of ourselves and schooled us to a different world. I stepped aside and married Delta. Trey? Maybe he's still waiting.

We stopped in front of Main Hall, paused and let more thoughts flow, then headed to the space that every small high school in Texas had...a "caf-a-gym-a-torium", confident that we would find a few faces we liked and sort through a lot more whose looks just didn't click, in high school or after. Those front-doors, wide open, let in old faces recreating stale fiction, and emptied hot air, recycling fresh. We would fit right in. Trey had plenty to talk about, and so did I, if someone wanted to ask.

I brushed up against Trice and Hamp, engaged in animated discussions about the basketball games we won, dismissing the ones we lost. Teammates then, and I visited with them briefly, making the only reference that reflected well of me. "Remember when we beat Marshall 100-72? School record. Still stands. You must'a been shooting a lot that night, Trice." He had the usual quick answer. "Hell, I was shooting every night…must'a been hittin-em." As everyone did, I let him have the last word, winked at Hamp and moved on into the crowd, having lost Trey to some other impulse.

The girls, now women, were on the left, near a large table, small purses in hand, or on an arm…posturing themselves as the makeweights of the evening…and who's to say they won't be. Their smiles flashed in the shadowed interior, and a good lip gloss and brushed cheeks painted their faces in ways that drew light in all the right places. They did look good, I had to admit, and a few "Hi Bobby," came my way as I wandered past. There were embarrassing histories in those looks, I knew, but tonight I didn't want to hear about my romantic failures or my clumsy efforts to find more skin than they wanted to reveal. I waved, smiled and connected…then moved on, faintly beginning to wonder where Trey had gone. Did he just go home? No. I heard a loud shout, deep in the semi-dark of the other deep corner. Loud laughter…Trey's… and his exclamation that bounced off every wall.

"SHONTEL! DAMN! I HOPED BUT…BY GOD, HALLO SHONTEL!"

39

She looked into the dark, knowing the voice, searching for the face, found him and walked in Trey's direction, shakin' her head like a rattle, letting the tail of her tightly drawn hair whip about her face, flashing the needles that I knew could be lethal. Her dress swirled loosely around her, showing those strong, lengthy legs in its shimmer, and she moved with the confidence of a female Moses parting a sea of faces. The closer she got to Trey, the wider his arms opened, and the more animated he became...and when she jumped into his body, he swung her as the merry-go-round would, skirt flaring, legs fluttering, joy animating every part of her body. Twice around. The circle ended. Trey sat her on her feet and just looked at her, and I had to say to myself, she's looking at him just as hard. Something's gonna happen tonight, and knowing what I knew about Shontel, it could happen anywhere.

A few more greets, a light kiss or two, a longer hug, and finally the two of them began to chat, the crowd melting away as it became clear where Shontel planned to spend her energy. I edged a little closer, hoping for an introduction, but determined to hear the soft talk.

"You been ignoring me a long time, White boy. Last I heard from you was a year now...you still buildin' shelters for the White folk on ocean views where shit don't flow on to the beaches...that right?"

Trey paused, thinking of how he might respond to this woman who had been in and mostly out of his life for the past three decades. What could he say? And while he paused to answer, another voice filled the void.

"HEY THERE NIGGER GIRL! YOU GOT A LITTLE ROOM FOR ME BETWEEN YOUR LEGS! LIKE ALL YOU ROSA PARKS GIRLS, YEAH?"

Instant silence...heavy silence...eyes searchin' to find the voice.

From out of the dark it came, harsh with liquor, roughened by anger, fueled by hate, dominance, and superiority, spitting in the face of human diversity.

"SHONTEL, SHONTEL BABY! WON'T YOU BE MINE? WE COULD BLEND SKIN AND TURN BLACK TO CHOCOLATE... THEN SHAKE IT UP...SHARE A SIP, EH, SHONTEL!

An anxious silence. A reunion with friends suddenly catapulted itself into racial drama, promising blood, assault, maybe murder, 'cause I knew Shontel still carried her pistol and those needles in her hair...and this figure I did not know was emerging out of the crowd, crossing the room toward her, gesturing one obscenity after another, sucking his lips, promising sexual adventures that belonged in a whorehouse.

The dude managed to get nearly 12 feet from Shontel, who was pulling her Derringer out without pause, when Trey reached him and what followed informed anyone who wondered what a blood fight was like. Distracted by his fixation on Shontel, the Mouth never turned toward the gliding shadow Trey cast...and what followed stunned Whites and Blacks alike. Trey shoved the dude enough to turn him toward himself, and as he came around, he hit him with an elbow, a thunderous 'CRACK' on his face, following immediately with a kick to his balls, and a karate chop to his neck. Trey grabbed his arm, twisted as he threw him and dislocated the shoulder. Went to kick his head in, when Shontel hollered, "NOUGH, TREY"! He stopped. Again, Shontel, "This tiny, teeny, flaccid weeny White boy is done. Let his friends just drag him out of here."

They did. Some members of the Reunion Committee brought out wet cloths to mop up the blood, as Trey carefully rearranged his clothing, walked over to Shontel, and looked her over carefully for sign of injury.

Took nearly twenty minutes for everyone to settle, then Trey tried to recreate the conversation they were starting before the interruption, remembered what she asked...about building homes... finally answered, "You asked about building homes, Shontel? Pretty much over that section of my life...plenty of money in the bank, just easin' myself into a bit of a float, lookin' for a new bend in the river."

The room was still so silent, we could all hear him declare his search for a "new bend in the river," and then Shontel's follow-up.

"Am I on that boat?"

She smiled with those eyes...damn those eyes, I thought. There won't be anything goin' on tonight besides Shontel...first the threat, then the fight, and now the magnetism of old high school lovers meetin' up one more time. Maybe that was all right.

Trey looked at her suddenly, differently. That comment, "Am I on it?" seemed to trigger a thought, maybe it was an impulse, but whatever, it energized him.

"Come on Shontel. let's find Bobby and the three of us can get in front of the photographer here and get our pictures taken for the reunion web site. Might be the best memory we'll ever have...speaking of...been in any movies lately, girl?"

Shontel's eyes dimmed just a bit. "Just waitin' for the right role, my tall tower of power." There was double entendre in those words, and she said them as though she knew what she was talkin' about, and I'm quite sure she did.

"You gonna be stayin over a day or so in Copa, or in Longview, where I suspect you can find a room nice enough for your nighttime antics?"

"Hadn't planned to...oh my God, there's Bobby," and she turned, spilling out that greeting that she seemed to have created just for me. "There you are, you bad, bad boy." She stepped toward me, that body of hers still flowing as did liquid soap, leaving a smooth trace of oil and promising a thorough cleansing...which I admit, I would have enjoyed. But still, there was Trey. No cue for me to confuse byplay with foreplay.

"I shoulda known you two would be in the same room, like always...lookin' for trouble, like always...and me sortin' things out to set you both on course again...like always. How'm I gonna be workin' my magic tonight after that Whitey guy done got stomped." She smiled brilliantly toward Trey. "Anyone else drunk or disorderly... send 'em to me and I'll calm 'em or twitch 'em...you know 'bout twitchin' Bobby?"

"I know horses, and I know twitchin', Shontel, and I'm sure there's things me and Trey would like to sort through with you...what I would call, 'Travels With Shontel'. Got stories?"

Trey interrupted, "Oh, I'm damn sure she does, lots of 'em, but let me bring this bullshit talk back to somethin' we touched on earlier, Shontel. Your career. You got anything under contract for the next year or so?"

"Oh, Trey, you know...I never plan ahead that far...just sortin' through options these days, lookin' for the right role."

"Well, then, hell, why don't you follow Bobby and me home tonight where we can provide you with clean quarters, a good night of fun and a breakfast of grits, eggs, cornbread and dark molasses... and when you've slept and done eatin' we might have a proposition for ya...and it wouldn't involve goin' back to bed, necessarily. Whaddya think?"

"S'up, White Boy? You got somethin' Shontel might want to be a part of? Convention hostess for a builder's convention or somethin' like that. I can sing, and I always look good, know what I mean?

Trey looked at me, a knowing look, and I knew why he wanted Shontel safe, clearheaded and well fed at our breakfast table the next morning.

Shontel. She might promise, and if she promised, as I remembered, she delivered. I looked into those eyes of hers, feeling a little lost, but still floating on the surface of her first look. I got into the conversation again.

"Shontel. Might be a lot of fun to talk about stuff...about futures. Whaddya think? Spend a day or so with us?"

She looked at me as though I were the sensible one, then at Trey who seemed to infatuate her with possibility, and she blended the two of us into a composite force that might work a little on her malleable form and turn a little clay into a bit of gold, and everyone likes gold... especially Shontel. She drew a deep breath, looked around the room and exhaled, smiled and said, finally, "Well, O.K., but it better be damn good cornbread."

CHAPTER 7

THE PITCH

If I become a tar baby for the critics, I will kill you both.
Shontel

Arlo told me once about moseying up to the mob. "Hard to be in business without protection, but once you get it, it's hard to walk away." Well, that saying stuck to me, and I could have said the same thing about Trey and Shontel. When a guy actually executes a beat-down to protect a girl…well, he's offering her something that is hard to ignore. After that fracas, I knew something was gonna happen with Trey and Shontel and once we got home, it did.

It wasn't a quiet night, nor did I expect one. I heard their sounds, the shouts and the pattern of the bed bumps. But I let my mind sort through other events of my history with her, some warm, a few disappointing, and concluded that only good could come from her and Trey mixing it up once again. I knew it made him happy, for now, but she never promised anyone a future.

Finally, sleep took me to the first crinkles of daylight. All quiet. I rose and started fulfilling the promise of cornbread. Took freshly ground meal, mixed it with buttermilk, salt and a little sugar and hoped that fit her palate. If Trey wanted her happy for talk about a movie, I would do my part. Dragged a fresh bottle of molasses out of storage, warmed it and then settled in for the arrival of my nighttime guests.

It took time, but I had plenty of it. I heard the two of them rustling at rising, even caught a slice of conversation that was decades old, "I told you long ago, Trey, havin' good sex is just that...not love. Go bring me my shower cap." A time of silence, then more murmurs, "I'm dressin' now, give me some air." And later, "Damn, Trey, don't this man have anything in a closet that doesn't have the word 'Delta' scrawled on it?" He mumbled an answer, and Shontel finally praised the Lord and pulled off what she described as a "goin' to Sunday church" dress. I wondered how it would fit.

The two slithered into the kitchen, still hiding grins, Shontel looking great in Delta's dress...as she would in anyone's. No doubt I'd be doing a wash later today, but for now...breakfast. Trey grinned at me, as happy as I have ever seen him, and they sat down to the best my kitchen could offer: scrambled eggs, pancakes, sausage patties, cornbread and molasses, topped with hot coffee. With every portion served, I thought of the symbolism of this meal...this gathering... this morning reconnaissance of options with Shontel. I could imagine selling my book for a streaming series. Maybe it would become a film booked into movie houses across the country. Perhaps a publisher would seek me out for another book...maybe a series. Sounds from the table balanced the audio in my head, and I waited.

Shontel finally pushed her scraps away, took a long swallow of coffee, looked me up and down, and turned to Trey.

"O.K. White boys. What you think you got me doing here, talkin' 'bout movies and such?"

I looked at Trey, raised an eyebrow, wondering whether there had been some pillow talk that took Shontel into our little world of HollyDreams. He said nothing to me...no sign at all. I waited, nodded to her and cued him to make the pitch.

"Well, woman," his voice, deep and rich, almost echoed throughout the kitchen, "I have some reading material for you to sift through and then Bobby and I want to have a conversation with you. Up for that?"

"You brought me here to eat cornbread...which incidentally I enjoyed, especially the buttermilk texture...and then you want me to sit and read a book. S'up?"

"You've read scripts and summaries of a pitch, eh Shontel. Look at the book Bobby wrote, and see how it fits your thoughts about a role in a film."

"Let me have a look."

Trey handed her a copy of WHY SHE WEPT and said, softly, "Have at it. We'll go take a walk and look at landscape and home sites for Bobby here. Get back in a couple of hours. You should be all be caught up by then."

He looked at me, nodded the door and out we went, Trey whispering in his gravelly voice, "Let's go see where you want me to build you a home." We drove to three different parts of my 2,000 acres, pausing at each to imagine the arc of the sun at different seasons, waterfront contrasts with small woodlands and protections from winds, likelihood of fire and general considerations of a home as a final resting place. I grew enamored with the idea of a site on Lake O' Pines, and as always, Trey had ideas, poking holes in some of mine, eliminating romantic ambiance for utilitarian sensibility, but keeping in mind the goal: easy steps into water, but privacy amidst seasonal crowds.

He asked me lots of questions: flat or stairs; glass or walls; attachments or single placement; materials...brick, wood, stucco, slats. We speculated on wells, septic systems, electric hook-ups, garden sites, driveway access, distance from main road. Basement as storm shelter? It went on and on and by the time we'd finished talking, the sun was past mid-day. Time to get back to Shontel, and I have to admit, either "Yes or No" would fit. The first meant I had a project. The second confirmed that I could continue to enjoy solitude and quiet.

We walked in the door, glanced at her curled up on the sofa, popping Red Flame hard candies, seemingly looking through the book to re-read specific parts, pausing a bit to stare off into space imagining, I am thinking, some particular scene and how she might play it. Was that encouraging to see...her mental engagement? Or was she trying to tell us why it was all ass-backwards and she saw nothing in it for herself. What was it Shontel? Help us out here. And she did.

"So, Bobby Banfield, you're an author, self-published, without a press to back you or a Fallon to hype you? Right?"

"Yep."

"And you wrote this book all by yourself...created the characters... supplied the dialogue...sorted out the plot?"

"Yep."

"Tell you the truth, I just sort of skimmed my way through a few chapters, and I'm not sure what to think of it. You believe I can play the role of who...the silent little bitch, Dottie the secretary... the slinky, classic-body lover, Suzanna...or the traitorous Chair of Psychology, Emma Watson? Whom I gonna be, Bobby Banfield?"

"None of 'em. We see you as the lead character, Sara Stone, Dean of Liberal Studies. She is hired because she's Black and told to fill the ranks of faculty with more Blacks. She is a deeply flawed person... sexually wide-ranging, carrying hidden ambitions to go along with her obvious limp, bad hearing, crippled hand and acrylic eye. In Trey's vision, she may not be a serial killer, but she is a cold-hearted bitch taking pleasure in human tragedy, flooded with hostility, trying to pass herself off as Black normal in a world full of White skeptics."

"You see me as a mess?"

"Shontel, we see you as the actress redefining herself in the role of a lifetime. Where you been the last ten years, eh? How many movies have you released? How many Broadway appearances have you made? How many specials on CNN or series on Netflix feature your name up on the title? I didn't see you in *House of Cards*."

"You didn't see any Black character in that series, Bobby. Edgy political drama for White folks. Nothing new for me."

"What have you been doin' that is new, Shontel? From my lookin', you've done a little bit of regional theatre, shown up in a few commercial promotions in Vegas, even tried out as a backup dancer on two Broadway musicals."

Trey picked right up. "Shontel. Think about what you're looking at here…a role we will write to fit you, a plot we can redesign to intensify the film, and money enough to send you cascading into all the night talk shows, along with the usual print in *Variety, Billboard, Starstruck, maybe a feature in Rolling Stone.*"

Shontel looked at him, eyes narrowing, no smile. "Where do you think your going to find that kind of money, Trey? You can treat a girl well enough, but I don't see you carrying enough bucks to restart my career. Don't you know the story about actresses of a certain age… they can't fill the wrinkles fast enough and the camera can't hide everything."

I wanted back into the conversation. "Shontel, what this country needs besides a strawberry shake from Denny's, is a movie that can address professional collegiate quibbling, indulge male sexual fantasy, whet the female appetite for protective drama, reveal the race war we are in, offend the sensibility of middle class values and make it all memorable…unforgettable. That is you. Audiences may not love Dean Sara Stone…will likely hate her…but they will never forget her."

"Do I look like a college Dean, Bobby? Really? I'm Black! Is there anything about me that shouts education, sophistication, specialized knowledge? What president of a college run by Whitey would hire a Black Dean? Eh? Think about it, boy."

"And that is the point, Shontel. Your character, Sara Stone, is a shallow hick from an Air Force family who made her way through college with Affirmative Action, hard work and a certain sexual strain of favors. The President of Middleton College knows of her from her work in the History Department. He's interested in selecting Deans who will be creative, hire Black faculty, and create a new racial balance. He wants the college to look a little like portions of St. Paul. He thinks Sara Stone might be able to do it. He is wrong."

"Why would that be, Bobby?"

"His Dean of AL&S (you), becomes a horror show. She speaks of her commitment to finding Black talent, hiring it and nurturing it whenever it shows up in faculty applicant lists. She means it, but becomes outraged with the indolence of departmental resistance. She is obstinate (you); she's sexually active (you); she has a temper and impulsive behavior (you); and finally, she has multiple handicaps."

"She's handicapped?"

"Yep...that artificial eye, bad knee, frozen fingers...all through a bike accident. Layer that on to her personality which is offensive to anyone looking for friendship...unless that someone is a lesbian, a male lover...or a connected academic, all of which can be you. Yet, she stands by the one principle for which she was hired...changing the color makeup of the faculty and creating a more diverse student body. This leads to trouble."

"Why trouble...sounds like our girlfriend is hitch-hikin' in the right direction."

"She is impatient, imposing change rather than leading it. She's flirting, fucking, and fighting her way through faculty hiring rules; she is obstructed by tenure protections, academic tradition and the challenge of dealing with her personal injuries. She finds herself fighting the only other Black faculty in a position of leadership."

"Who's that?"

"Chair of the English Department, Monique Baroque'. She's not in the book. I'm adding her to the narrative, cause we need an anti-hero. Monique, ebony skinned as she is, identifies herself as a White person, rejects Dean Sara Stone's agenda and focuses on recruiting poor Whites."

"How's that gonna' go down in the Big House?"

"Not well."

"Anything else 'bout this Dean lady..what's her name?"

"Dean Sara Stone. Yes, there is one other issue. She is a trans-gender woman who has not come out."

"WHAT! How'd I miss that a-skimming? Hmmmm. Well, Bobby Banfield, that ain't the 'other issue'. That's the main branch upon which I can hang my hook! Transgender, eh? Hiding it from faculty and all? Bet I'm gonna be practicing my craft on both men and women, Black and White? Oh my soul! I'm excited! How's that gonna' work out?"

"Not well."

"Oh, I would think not. My Lord, Bobby do-right…that girl's gonna get battered! You're thinking a Black woman can change White America and all that and still rest easy in her chair? Say boy, do Dean's have chairs, or is it department's have chairs?"

"Dean's have chairs, those they sit in and those they control, monitoring power and access to every nuance of university life. They can create, destroy, nurture and starve lives, careers and romance. Powerful enough for you?"

"Maybe. But what 'bout this raging academic terrorist is personal to the character?"

"It's as personal as it can get, Shontel. She's infatuated with power, but has an array of flaws, physical and emotional. She's often flatulent, politically ruthless, and lives with an acrylic eye which she cleans frequently, as she limps about dragging a bad leg…a Quasimodo in cap n' gown. She's sexually active with men and women, professors and secretaries, and, some would say, students of a certain ilk. Dean Sara Stone is sometimes murderous and always dangerous."

"You want me to be farting on screen, screwing women, bedding men, killing people, dictating course contents, limping around sending faculty types running for air? That right, Bobby?" She smiled. "I gotta say that appeals to me?"

"We want a great actress to make a character so repulsive, the audience cannot get her misdeeds out of their minds. Six months after seeing you, viewers will still be shuddering and that's long enough."

"You think I'm it, Bobby Banfield? Hmmm…been a few Black women starring in some big time movies, lately, but none like this. How's that gonna be, a Black girl running things, controlling faculty, meeting secret lovers in the auditorium and what-not? You think America's gonna bond to that?"

"A great performance is a great performance, Shontel. Think of Viola Davis in *Fences*. How about Halle Berry in *Monster's Ball*, taking home the Oscar…first Black woman to hold it. 'Bout Queen Latifah in *Chicago*, eh? Go back to Josephine Baker, Lena Horne. Great performers…Black women…they are in the mix, and you're sitting here…today…ready to make tomorrow."

She looked a little more open to the idea, but still unconvinced. I tried harder.

"Great actresses manage mixed messages, Shontel. In her day, Ann-Margaret could romance both Elvis and an old man, Walter Matthau, on screen and everyone felt right at home following her winning smile and hot pants. You're a far better actress than Ann-Margaret, right Shontel?"

"No comparison, Bobby Banfield. No pixie-eyed set of teeth is gonna outshine Shontel...I'll be new to the view and wet to pet," she laughed, went on, "And I guess there's gotta be something that's really evil in the character, cause when she dies, we don't want tears. We want satisfaction...people walking out of the theatre saying she got what she deserved! Some of it I can understand, but a transgender dean letting young boys and old men die...makes even me want to vomit. That right my sweet young man?"

"As Trey and I look at it, she offends everyone and is in constant peril."

"She gonna live?"

"We don't know yet."

Unless my stares deceived me, Shontel was now buying in, thinking like a director, instructing script and interpreting the character of a star...herself. I encouraged her. "Your performance will stick in viewer's minds for months, Shontel. When we finish our hype, your face will be imprinted on the minds of millions of movie fans, and by the by, you will have made a lot of money. If we start now, when the Academy hands out Oscar a few years from now, you'll be in the audience with a seat of your own."

(I paused, leaving that thought floating in her mind).

She looked intensely at each of us, searching for the cut, the disrespect, the foolishness that White men often hide when dealing with Black women. She didn't see that. Still, there was doubt.

"If a Black woman can be a Dean, a murderer and a sexual explorer, what's gonna keep people from asking if she isn't just Black scraps?" She turned to Trey. "I don't see stardom in that, do you?"

Trey stayed right in the loop. "Shontel, a star remains a star, even in decline. With the right role, she can draw on the memories of what she once was, and without blinking an eye, drag the viewer into what she now is. A great actress can allow the audience to remember the old and embrace the new. A great actress can turn scraps into steak…and Shontel…you are a great actress."

Silence. I started to keep the pitch rolling, then thought better of it. Let her digest all this hype…and her candies.

She took her time, glancing from time to time to look at our faces, popping a Red Flame or two, reading our moods, re-reading a passage or two and convincing herself we were serious and she should be too. I finally got up and brought Trey some paper, a ruler and a No. 2 pencil which I knew he didn't prefer, but it was all I had. "Draw some ideas 'bout this house you plan to build me, Trey. It may well be finished before Shontel makes up her mind."

Trey roughed in some specs and brief descriptions. The windows were large, tinted, rationing light. A spacious kitchen. Two bedrooms, cause I really don't want a lot of company…and the lines went on, letting my new home emerge, and offering me comfort for the brief stint of years ahead. "We'll talk some more on this, Trey. I'm gonna go sit out on the porch."

I got up to leave, and as I turned, Shontel said, quietly. "I'll do it. I'll do it, but if I become a tar baby for White folk critics…if I end my career with this shit, then Trey, my tall, tall man, and Bobby, my bad, bad boy…(she paused)…I will kill you both."

She wasn't smiling.

CHAPTER 8

HOOKING UP

Sometimes, out of the blue, a look will do.
Bobby Banfield

We had our actress. What we needed now was a screenplay to pitch to moneymen. Trey didn't have any suggestions, but I did. When I founded the School of Theatre and Film at Middleton College, I made sure it was run by a professional with one foot in Broadway and the other in Hollywood. And each time there was a faculty vacancy, I hired real talent, not talent agents. I wasn't sure who was running ST&F now, but whoever it was could likely help us find a screenwriter. With nothing to do at Bar Delta, I left Trey to curry favor with Shontel, flew to Minneapolis, caught an Uber over to Middleton College and went looking for the Dean.

Olivia Downey sat on a stone, memorial bench eating a small, egg sandwich, sipping her favorite mid-day drink, ice-coffee, and mulling her annual budget. Dean of the *School of Theatre and Film*, she carried her responsibility stylishly, felt its weight daily. The Trustees were exploring "programmatic adjustments" as they called it, a term cloaking a terrorist raid on her budget. She knew that game, and she knew ST&F survived, sketchily, by exporting its reputation to the foundations attached to New York Theatre and Los Angeles Studios.

Converting reputation into cash...that was always the dilemma. She didn't have the answers for this year...yet...but she would find them.

She arose, took a final swallow, tossed the cup into the metal trash container next to her and began the walk back to the office. Lazily, she ran a mental montage of her daily tangles: faculty protests about programming, new versus traditional; maintenance, maybe some repairs on the new theatre; the bi-annual requests for grants which became a toxic seduction of all things academic. She had a wish, an easy wish. She wished she were Cuba Gooding, jr.

Playing the role of the pro football player, Rod Tidwell, Gooding could shout *"Show Me the Money!"* and everyone knew his truth. Even Tom Cruise could not slither away from that demand. It was a clear standard of accomplishment that had to be met and Gooding never let him off the hook. Now, sorting through her departments, her chairs, her actors, performers, singers and dancers, Olivia wondered how she could balance quality and dollars this year. That she would, she had no doubt. But how? Performance was one thing, but unlike Rod Tidwell's life, roaring crowds did not produce cash, only a certain smug satisfaction that the acting community had done its work... moved the audience, hilariously or tearfully...as it should. No extra payment required. She needed to work on that.

Her cell buzzed. She picked up to hear the voice of Elise Clayton, her secretary, quietly conveying a message. "Olivia, there's a guy in my office introducing himself as the former President of the college, and he says he wants to meet with you."

"Former President?"

"Yes. Dr. Robert Banfield."

Olivia paused, trying to reference Banfield into her memory, finally realized he left a couple of years before she was hired as Dean. She grimaced. Nothing in her professional life irritated her more than old-timers skittering around the campus after pronouncing to the world they were leaving it. Now, here was President Robert Banfield, retired, seeking her out, no doubt with some suggestions to help her right a "floundering" ship, one which, however leaky, she believed seaworthy for the decade ahead. Still, he had created the STF, insisted on its development and always took personal interest in it. So, what now?

"Be nice, Elise, and welcome him home to the university. Tell him I am across campus but on my way to meet him. Give him one of your nice smiles."

"Easily done, Olivia. He's a treat to see." A quiet laugh accompanied her words. Well, Elise did have an eye for men, Olivia thought, but God forbid this guy wants us to get involved in his pet project. Last thing she needed was an old-timer trying to fiddle with her budget for next year's performance schedule.

She turned off her cell, put the sandwich wrapper and coffee cup in the trash sack hanging from the nearby post and headed to the office. "Bobby Banfield." That's the way people referred to him, she remembered. As she walked, she quietly snapped her fingers, keeping time with every other step. Maybe it would be a friendly meeting. She trudged a bit crossing campus, still mulling how to raise more dollars from a battered public and an unenthusiastic administration. Reached the doors to the theatre...had a thought. Wondered if Bobby Banfield had any money...maybe he wanted to see his name on a building? So distracted was she with this thought that she entered the main office without glancing at Elise, or the man sitting gracefully in a large, red sofa.

As she closed the door and swung around, her skirt twirled nicely, accentuating her calf and a very trim ankle. Bobby Banfield noticed. Caught himself wondering why he had any reaction at all and waited for Dean Olivia Downey to find him. She searched the room, landed on him and immediately felt a little pulse in her throat. She had not expected to see what filled that sofa...a trim, well groomed fellow, casually dressed, fashionably bald,...a man who looked to be 55, but could be less. He looked up as she paused in her review, and she caught his blue eyes, sparkling, a soft smile on his face and puzzlement about what he saw.

"Well, Dean Downey. Good morning! So nice of you to come in from the cold, so to speak, and visit an old-timer who almost surely has nothing but trouble on his mind."

She paused, not sure how to engage this candid banter...not sure how to set aside her impulsive reaction to the man speaking to her. For an ex-president, he seemed casually correct, openly engaging, and if her years of experience were not betraying her, he liked the way she looked. "Ditto", she thought.

"President Banfield, Bobby Banfield, and is it ok for me to just call you 'Bobby'?" She was blathering, and she didn't quite know why. She waited for a reply.

"And Dean Downey, could I assume a friendship familiar enough to call you, "Olivia"?

She nodded a yes and with a wave of her hand motioned him into her office, followed, and quietly closed the door...an unusual gesture, Elise thought. She didn't know Banfield and neither did Olivia. Yet they were going to be having private conversations based on a moment's recognition. Sweet. On impulse, she cancelled the rest of the Dean's appointments for the day.

Olivia chose to sit in the visitors hard chair, welcomed him into the more comfortable sofa lining the wall and offered him a beverage. "Coffee, tea or me" she thought and then thought better of it, "Care for a drink, Bobby." The game was on, just like that.

"No, I'm fine, Olivia." Yes, that felt comfortable and it felt good. What's next.

"And why are you back on campus? I think I arrived a couple of years after you retired, but I never heard much about your departure other than you seem to have just played out your interest in the job. Is that right?"

"It is. I have always believed that every professional assignment has a shelf life. A beginning, filled with energy and creative ideas; a middle, putting together all the pieces of the vision and managing it through infancy; an end, when projects are mature, running themselves and one wonders what to do next, and the answer is 'Find Something Else'. At that time, I was brushing past 50, my wife, Delta, had developed ALS and I figured it was time to get out before someone pushed me. We retired to a homestead she inherited from her Dad, near Longview, Texas. I turned my attention to grass, cows and horses. Loved it there, still do, though it's a bit empty without her. Been awhile...just recently decided to sign up for the human race again."

Silence.

Olivia, listening intently, scrutinized Bobby's face without ever moving her head. She heard his tone, his voice reciting a memory, not reliving a tragedy...healthy...saw the liveliness in his body language... liked everything she felt radiating from his smile, his intonation, his posture, and simply thought to herself, "I'm interested".

Bobby felt the care with which she seemed to be listening. Something in his gut stirred, just a bit, enough to tell him to be careful about how he told his story. Wanted to tell it well.

Olivia picked up his account, "So, one day, down in Longview, Texas, Bobby Banfield just up and flew to Middleton College, to drop in to see the Dean of the School of Theatre and Film without a warning or an appointment. How'd that happen?"

Bobby sorted through his message once again, decided against it, and just went with what he wanted to say. "I need a screenwriter."

"What?"

"I need to prepare a screenplay for a film I'm producing, based on a book I've written, WHY SHE WEPT. In turn, the book was based on my experiences with my Dean of AL&S, Dean Jeanette Swift. You have surely heard of her shenanigans with her college and the multiple efforts made to kill her. Pretty dramatic stuff."

"Hmmm. I heard something about her...two appointments ago I think, and no one spoke well of her...guess there was a reason, eh?"

"Well, I thought so. In real life, I had to govern through all of it, picking up the mess she created, and I hated it...diverting my energies to what I call 'slut work'. Another good reason to get out of town. We had that haven in Texas, and I figured we would settle in for Delta's decline, mine to follow."

"And yet, here you are."

"Sometimes, out of the blue, opportunity disturbs equanimity."

"Bobby Banfield, I have a hard time believing anything happens to you 'out of the blue'. Still, you are here, and amidst our fun little talk, I have a feeling that you have a well designed purpose. Eh?"

"I do. As I said, I need a screenwriter. I thought I would see if you could help me find one."

"What's the screenwriter gonna do for you?"

"Take my book, WHY SHE WEPT and convert it to a film-worthy narrative. That's what screenwriters do, don't they? Do they do more?"

The nuance of that last question, caught Olivia in mid-breath, and she liked the short feeling it produced. "Bobby Banfield...you flirting with me?"

"If you think I am...I am."

"You sure you want to be doin' that?"

"More certain every time you speak."

He looked at her, locked eyes, took in her lines and smiled as she glowed a bit. She returned the smile, sent a bit of electricity toward him, cleared her throat.

"Let me see your book, Bobby."

"Two things."

"Yes?"

"The lead will be played by Shontel Williams, a Black actress, who will play Sara Stone, a Black woman isolated in her collegiate community. Another character, one not in the book, will be another Black woman, Monique Baroque', Chair of the English Department. She will be Sara Stone's antagonist."

"Well, fairly warned. Let's see it."

She held out her hand. He slipped the book to her, pages intact, cover crisp. As Olivia took it, she touched his hand, an incidental contact, but one shocking them both. She looked up as she grasped the book, saw his eyes focused on her, met them without hesitation and held the look…long enough.

They both now knew there was more than a book review driving their conversation. There was a magnetism, the kind that, without warning, stirs the gut, sends a tickle to the heart and dries the throat. He was a little stunned. Not a thought of Delta. Not a whim about the reverie of Longview. Not a sense of guilt…only the sudden parting of the wispy cloudiness that had drifted across his feelings for the past couple of years.

Olivia felt the book grow hot in her hand, light perspiration forming as she struggled to keep control of her rising body warmth. "Stay cool and professional," she cautioned herself, even though she knew, as she knew Bobby Banfield knew, this conversation would not end over a book…or a screenplay…or a polite thanks for taking up some time.

"Well, Bobby," she looked straight into his eyes, silently snapping her fingers in a slow cadence. "Why don't we have a meal together this evening and talk about this project?"

He felt the hook, let it sink in and quietly responded, "I think that would be the best 'end of the day' I have had in quite some time, Olivia. Can I ask you to chose a restaurant. I've been away awhile."

"I'll treat you to *Druids*," she replied, certain the atmosphere, the food and the ambiance was just what she wanted. "It's up on the Bluffs, where life begins about 8 pm each evening. Sound o.k.?"

"I'll find it." And now he knew it was time to leave. Slightly confused with his feelings, brightened with Olivia's willingness to look at the book, and smitten...there was no other word for it, he thought...smitten with her looks, her personality, her being. He wanted more.

So did she.

He rose, dared not touch her hand again, bowed slightly (such a cute curious gesture, she thought), and turned to leave, letting his words float behind him. "See you this evening, young lady."

And that was the question, she thought. "Young Lady". Just how young was she. Just how much older was he...the age difference. Did it matter? As she mentally calculated, Bobby Banfield, was in his early 50s...about. She was 43. Sex was definitely on the table, as she might be herself, depending on what tonight brought. Was he too old to sustain the edge, the hunger? Well, what long-term relationship could? Hot to start, cool to warming temperature within a year or two...or three. Enough! Why was she thinking long term with Bobby Banfield? No answer, but she told Elise to cancel the rest of her appointments and hurried home. She laughed about this sudden urgency to feather her next, and flitted about her apartment cleaning small tables, scrubbing scents, tidying the kitchen, adjusting the indoor lighting...just in case. Thoughts about him took her sorting through selections of dress, scent and jewelry for the evening. Finally, in a desperate move to get herself on track, she sat down and skimmed his book, WHY SHE WEPT. It was engaging, exuded a certain sexual energy and she found herself caught up in the killings and the solution to murder. Had possibilities. She could even envision the logline for the movie.

TITLE: QUICKSILVER. *A Black, Transgender Dean plays "Who Can You Trust" with her White faculty.*

O.K. The book they could talk about. The sex would be a little more complicated...but wasn't it always.

He got lost only once making his way up the narrow road, but delighted in Druid's views reaching twinkling lights across the river. Not the devil's lair, exactly, but a haven for the devil's work. Nice setting for multiple moods, he thought and warmed when Olivia greeted him in the lobby a little after 8 o'clock. She inquired about the reservation, and they were seated immediately, he guiding her to follow the maitre'd with a gentle grasp around her waist. "Oh my God," she thought, "There it is again." Electricity.

They sat. Bobby ordered a Cab, along with appetizers...fried squash, boiled chunks of lobster and a French bread that held both crisp crust and scented yeast...small scoops of butter on the side. They chatted aimlessly while enjoying the wine...school enrollments, climate in Longview, lack of salary, embarrassment of land riches...all informative and all irrelevant to the purpose of the evening.

With the bottle gone and a Pinot Noir on the way, he paused, finally leaned forward and spoke to Olivia with his eyes, and with his voice.

"I know what we're doing here, tonight, Olivia. My only guidance is this, "When it's over, move on. I don't forgive a dalliance on the side, and I won't engage in one."

"Well, Bobby Banfield," she thought, "We have thoughts we can share, a rule I can embrace, and an evening to do anything we want... and save the book for tomorrow." She looked at him, nodded, said, "Do we have to wait for the French Dip?"

He brought out a roll of cash, pealed off two $100 bills, and left them on the table, drew back the curtain, caught the attention of their waitress and slipped out of the booth. "We've decided we need to be somewhere else," he murmured, "The tip is for you; keep the Pinot Noir for yourself. We won't be ordering."

Olivia didn't remember much about the night after that...only that her appetite was larger than she had believed, and she discovered a man in his early 50s could still ring her bell again...and again.

CHAPTER 9

QUICKSILVER

A film has to stir emotions, create tension, reflect choices...got to.
Olivia Downey

Everything about awakening with Olivia worked. She liked to sleep late, as did I. She slept in light clothing. She liked sex at night and in the afternoon, and that fit my body tempo just fine. But perhaps best of all, she liked to talk, liked to share ideas, liked to challenge mine, and she brought a lifetime of experience to a task...writing a screenplay...about which I was ignorant.

We let Trey know we would be working a few weeks to bring him a draft for editing and review, and I began trying to imagine how a movie about my newly named character, Sara Stone, might look. How would it differ from my novel, WHY SHE WEPT? How much would the storyline change, to fit drama on screen as opposed to mystery in a book? Lots of questions.

Olivia took two days, when she was free of me, reading the novel again, and then once again. I liked to believe she was dallying so as to keep me courting her with all the cues I could muster. Maybe so. Maybe not. Sometimes she silently clicked her fingers, as though creating a timing mechanism that would apply to the dynamics in the book. Other times, she was making notes, turning pages, re-reading passages, professionally evaluating its screen potential, staring in space, imagining. She finally asked me to have a session to work through ideas, and I drew a sigh. At last. We sat in her living room, filling comfortable, well cushioned chairs, iPads in our laps, ready to exchange comments and record notes.

I looked at her, "O.K., Olivia, this is your show. Where do we begin?"

"First thing to remember, Bobby, is that this is a movie. It is not a play being filmed. It is not a book put to film. It is a creation in its own right, and it will have rules and pitfalls as occur with any other creative production. Dialogue will be sparse. Very sparse. Film is a visual medium presenting scenery, recording faces at different angles, people walking from one placement to another, bodies posturing, lengthy pauses in dialogue, changing tempos, looks that fill the screen, character interactions...and a screenplay needs to incorporate those aspects of film as it translates the subject of the book."

"Meaning, I take it, that I may not like what you are doing to the fictional treatment of my murder mystery?"

"Exactly. So, in my opinion, your best strategy is to help create the screenplay. If you're in on the ground floor, you're more likely to like the rooftop."

"Well, then, I mentioned to you a little earlier this idea of a new character...not in the book. I see her as a Black woman who is Chair of the English Department. I think we need another Black face in the conversation about power, curriculum and such."

"I remember and I agree. I've worked something out in my notes, so we'll take a look at that."

"And with Monique in the story, you have ideas on how to keep me happy...as an author of a book which will become the basis for a screenplay which will then turn into a movie?"

"I do."

"Got notes?"

"I do."

"Let's hear 'em."

"You sure?"

"Yep."

"OK, I'm gonna begin with the title. As you'll see we really will not be concerned about why anyone wept. Your novel told a story of intense misbehavior and exaggerated arrogance in a middle-aged, White woman, carefully concealing her transgender status, ambitious for a college presidency and willing to put herself in any sexual position to get it."

"Yep."

"When the reader believed she had been murdered, you set up a conundrum. Who did it?"

"I thought the answer was pretty clever, eh?"

"It was, Bobby. But now, she's dead. Do we care? Maybe not so much."

"Why not?"

"Bobby, the novel was a nicely constructed letdown. A bit of fun, certainly. A mild vent on the idiocy of college faculty and administrators? Yes. But at the end, what do you have left? Ho hum."

"Well, grant me that it was well-written and a pleasant read, do you think?"

"Well, sure. Something like having sex with a friend. Nice ride, but it wouldn't take you 'cross the prairie. And that is the flaw of the book. It's tiresome. *WHY SHE SLEPT* has to be reconfigured into something like *QUICKSILVER*."

"What! Really...really? And...just thinking, Olivia...isn't Quicksilver the name of a film...back in the 80's sometime."

"Might be, but who cares. We're not naming racehorses. I like the title. It promises a little mystery and a lot of slippery behavior. Focus here, Bobby! You tell me Shontel is your star. The movie is in large part a vehicle for her to stun the dramatic world with her performance."

"Yep, it is."

"Well, then we better do something to heighten tension, give her a role she can chew on...take advantage of this talent you see in her."

I took a breath. "O.K., Olivia...just lay it out for me."

"Well, first thing we have to do is reset the story line. A successful film needs *irony* in its climactic scenes. Without it, an audience will find the whole storyline too pat, too predictable, trite."

"So, my Black Dean, Sara Stone, is gonna have to die some other way?"

"Well, maybe not. All her flaws, her weaknesses, her assaults on the integrity of her relationships and her dismissal of faculty respect... all of it...will beg for her death...and the viewer is going to anticipate someone killing her...will wait for the moment she rolls her good eye and collapses into a bowl of thick soup."

"And?"

The two questions are: will it be done and who is going to do it? If she dies, could her killer be her lover, Suzanna, or her secretary Dottie? Perhaps it could be her arch-enemy, Betsy Moran, Chair of Psychology? Might it be Monique Baroque', Chair of English, this new character you're adding?"

"You feel ok about her...Monique?"

"Yep. I have a delightful idea on how to use her. You'll see why."

Olivia paused, and hell, even I became a little antsy. What in the dramatic world was gonna happen next. Olivia's voice rose, "Again, my query, Bobby. Who's gonna kill Sara Stone? Who's gonna get rid of her?"

She paused and just looked at me. I ventured a guess. "Doesn't matter. When she dies, the movie ends with justice administered. The world has been saved again. Right?"

"No," Olivia was very precise about the next few sentences. "The world is not going to be at peace. Sara Stone will mystify. Does she live? Does she die? The audience won't know, exactly."

"My God, what kind of climactic justice is that? How is the audience going to relate to her if her demise is ambivalent?"

"We're not making a movie about justice achieved. We're making a film about justice postponed, perhaps denied."

"Well, does anyone die?"

"Absolutely!

"Sara Stone gonna' do it?"

"Yep, she can murder a older man about to change his will, removing the Foundation in favor of his children. She can ignore a drowning child for fear of being identified in a public place with her lover, Suzanna. She can even kill her most personal secretary, Dottie, BUT, and this is important...maybe she doesn't get caught."

"Where's the drama in that, Olivia...a killer still on the loose? Eh?"

"The drama is in the leaving, Bobby. Ending a story with one loose end, whets the audience, stirs conversation, produces gossip about the film. That's what you want... gossip, exclamation, some outrage."

"That's a lot dying for just gossip. What else?"

"She guts personal and professional relationships, leveraging them to increase her academic power."

"Any die-hard enemies?"

"Several."

"What about Monique Baroque'? What can you do with her?" I was getting a little nervous about how to use this new character. I believed the story needed her, but how?

"So here she is, this Monique, eh? Department Chair...that's gonna be a problem for Sara Stone. Way I see it, Bobby, Monique's smart and eloquent, but ebony skinned as she is, she identifies as White, and speaks flawless English. Now, let me be clear about this...Monique does not 'pass for White'. She *identifies* as White. In her mind, she <u>is</u> White, much as a trans-gender person identifies as a different sexual being. Monique recognizes early on that Dean Sara Stone is a near-desperate, ambitious, ruthless, career crushing package of horror. No one else seems to see this, but Monique does…and undermines Stone's curriculum plans at every opportunity."

"Curriculum outrage? Really? That gonna be the basis for murder?"

"Personnel follows curriculum, Bobby. Power follows personnel. That is why Monique is such a problem. She is a Black face in a world of White, able to segue from Black Rap, "cap your ha'id in dat rag", to White Polite with comments such as "pardon me" or a vigorous, "I cannot agree." Her identity is a problem for the audiences…when have they confronted a Black woman who speaks as a self-identified White professor, eh? She is an outrageous figure to liberals and a gut-wrenching contradiction to conservatives…and she is a problem for Sara Stone."

"How so?"

"She raises money aplenty, enough to embarrass Stone, but a more serious issue is her attack on English grammar."

"Eh?"

"Sara is vomiting enmity over Monique's effort to raise the issue of gender-based pronouns used in writing, reading and analyzing literature."

I interrupted, "Gender based what?"

"Pronouns…think of it as a guerrilla attack on formal English. Instead of identifying a person as 'he' or 'she', one simply refers to a person in non-gender specifics, as in 'they'."

"So, they and they went to the movies?"

"Well, probably you can just say, 'They went to the movies'. The word can be either plural or singular, just non-specific as to gender."

"Who's doing this? Anyone?"

"*Washington Post* is about to make it a part of its standard usage; AP is considering it, as is Merriam-Webster."

"Sort of undermines what English is all about, eh?"

"Well, depends on who you are, doesn't it?"

I postured. "Language is for commonly shared methods of communication, not individual eccentricity."

"Well, Bobby, think of the community as a living body that includes little exceptions all through itself: moles, skin barnacles, warped limbs, bald heads, tattoos, scars. Every body is human; but every body is different...or to be cute about it, *every body is not everybody*. New pronouns allow each person to reference themselves without feeling different. That's what you would be doing."

"What I would be doing is inconveniencing myself. Why would I want to do that?"

"To make someone feel better."

"I'm gonna pass on that one, Olivia. You feeling' ok with 'she'?"

"Always."

"What's this about the money?"

"Monique can raise money and it ends up where it belongs."

"Sara Stone cannot raise money?"

"Oh, she can. She raises it promising to build a Foundation for the college and deepen its resources, describing the arrival of a flood of Black students from the inner cities and holding out the lure of career salvation for the underprivileged."

"And she does this why?"

"To show good faith."

"Does it work?"

"In a limited way. She imports a few Chicago Blacks, but that's just for show. For the dough, she contracts for a two-story, creatively designed building for the Foundation, hosts a 'talent' search for

Milwaukee minorities, to no effect, but great publicity. She squanders the bulk of the pledges on personal travel, rewarding friends and puffing up the space and furnishings of her office. There are questions about Foundation balances, and Monique Baroque' is among the skeptics."

"What else is going on in Sara Stone's world?"

"She's also challenged by Betsy Moran, Chair of Psychology."

"What's Betsy gonna do? And why?"

"She's gonna do just as you wrote. She will defend her department and her faculty by threatening a review of Stone's plans before the Faculty Senate, perhaps an appeal to the Board of Regents, but she will not give Stone one moment of peace...and why should she? Her department is being threatened. She thirsts for vengeance and her life begins to focus on dismantling Stone, professionally and personally."

"Coming back to Monique. How does she fit in to an improved faculty?"

"Not so much. She is an embarrassment to the entire college... imagine an educated, verbal, eloquent Black woman who identifies as White, representing the English Department. What the hell does that do for racial equity? If only Sara Stone could get rid of her...and she thinks about it from time to time...but Monique does raise a lot of money to help poor Whites living in the rural pits of Minnesota. And she insists on teaching Black students White English and White idiom. Nothing bad about that...it's the path toward success in the business world. Maybe, in a ass-backwards sort of way, Monique is a force for integration. Eh?"

"I guess. So, Sara lets her remain head of the English Department. Why?"

"Because living in Minnesota Nice, she identifies as White, sounds White...but she looks Black. Perfect."

"Well, Olivia, somewhere in there is some of my novel. If you're writing the screenplay maybe we can film something that Shontel and Trey will love...and maybe we'll find a director we like too."

"Speaking of directors, Bobby..."

"Yeah...what about 'em."

"I'm gonna give you a list of four or five I think can make this film special. You, Shontel and Trey can choose whoever appeals. But he, or she, or they...she smiled at that... is gonna have to interact well with Shontel and be able to keep the film on schedule. There will be delays, reasonable delays, and the monied people need to have reserves...be malleable. But in the end, the director has to produce a film bearing close resemblance to what has been written, and what investors have been promised."

"Are these names A-List?"

"Well A-/B+, but they can deliver you a film that has integrity, drama, revulsion, and in the end, irony."

I paused...tried to mentally wrap myself around the metamorphosis of my book into this anger-laced, racist, lethal drama. Olivia's twists were substantive, penetrating. Shontel would have the freedom to pursue her dramatic self and that could give us a box-office winner all by itself.

"Olivia. You mentioned earlier that Shontel would have a few scenes that could catapult her into the awards season. What are they?"

"You'll see. My question is, "Will Shontel buy into this?"

"She will love it."

CHAPTER 10

A NEW ROLE

Ride the wave, honey. You never know when it's gonna break.
Shontel

With Bobby gone, Shontel and Trey settled in. A couple. Intimates. Keeping house. For how long, she wondered, would this little play drama continue and what did it mean to her? Rarely had she kept company with any man or woman in a single setting for more than a week. Her nature, and her raising told her to avoid commitments she could not keep, and through the decades she found pleasure in moving on to new highs before a low set in.

She kept her eye on Trey, not so much because she worried or feared him, but because she did not want an emotional fallout if she decided to abruptly leave...which is how she usually departed an affair. But she didn't hold that feeling now, and she found it difficult to define their time together as a love-in...more like a natural homecoming without a schedule. And as she had for many years, she decided to go with what seemed to be working, what seemed to feel best, and play it to the limit. Leaving was always easy. Just pack a bag and take a walk.

In this new environment, free to explore one another without the slightest concern about who was listening or taking space in the home, they fell into a new rhythm: sleeping late, breakfast for lunch; reading *Variety, Dallas News* and the *N.Y Times*; chattering about celebrities, architectural challenges, and life in general. Walks along the lakefront or into the gently elevated pines, found them holding hands, enjoying breezes and birds, chatting about a highlight in Shontel's career or one of Trey's successful urban designs. She took note that her usual hesitation in being outdoor with bugs, dirt, or snakes disappeared and she set aside her caution at being seen side by side with a White man.

"What's go'in on here, Trey. We been havin' lots of fun in and out of bed. Why do I want to go walkin' with you? Not my usual style, showin' White men in public. Nobody sees me in bed."

"You think its risky? Eh?"

"It's Texas."

"You still carrying that Derringer?"

"Always."

"Let's go."

They also took a canteen of water, and a handful of Red Flame hard candy, something Shontel kept at arm's reach most of her quiet times. As they strolled, she would pop a nugget, sweeten thoughts, look at him...absorb him...just walking, talking.

"Shontel. What are you all about? No one has the professional success you've had without drive and energy. I see your talent, but what don't I see about you, eh? What makes you tick?"

"Take a good look, Trey. I'm Black. You're White. We're in Texas and the chains of lovin' and livin' life are pretty much fixed. You know how I was raised."

"I know your mama was a guide and an inspiration. What don't I know?"

"We grew up poor, transient, colored and discarded...my daddy moved around a lot lookin' for work, findin' shelter, feedin' us. But, he never abandoned us. I could feel that. And I enjoyed my schoolin'... Rosa Parks High...great name, easy teachers, poor buildin's. But restlessness was just born into me, I guess. I always wanted more...

more recognition, more praise, more money, more goods...more high living."

"Never seemed to bother you when we were dating. You seemed to take it all in stride...and when you felt ready, I guess...you left one world behind and explored another. Half my friends used to think you were a mulatto tryin' to fit into the White world 'round you."

"Truth be told, Trey, the White world looked a hell of a lot more interesting."

"Don't know that we were. My family was a mess...violent, uneducated, prejudiced about every name that wasn't theirs. I'd have traded that for some of your mom's views on life...what I learned from her through you helped me all through my younger days. She was known for her work as a voodoo fortune teller, wasn't she? That always sounded pretty phony to me, but you were always so 'feet in the dirt' grounded. You feel the same?"

"Oh sure...I used to love sneakin' round her little dark room, sometimes makin' little noises to get the "marks" gaspin' and believin'. Mama loved it and her truth-tellin' 'bout life hit me square and center every time. Dressing clean and crisp; eatin' right; lookin' good; knowing 'bout sex; listenin' to my teachers. I didn't do much with that last rule, but I liked 'em."

"Sex education...you sayin'?"

"No, White boy, 'bout sex...and also about education."

"What she sayin' bout' dat?"

"You soundin' like me, Trey...stop it!" She nudged his side with her elbow...it hurt.

"Well, what did your mother teach you about these things?"

"She taught me first of all about sex...why it's there, what its for and how to manage it."

"And what were the answers?"

"Well, it's there 'cause God put it there...to be used for three purposes...makin' babies, havin' pleasure and breakin' hearts."

"I don't hear anything there about virginity, saving oneself, fidelity, truth, love and the American way," Trey smiled.

"That's White man talk, Trey. Nobody believes that bullshit once the clothes come off. She taught me 'bout birth control, safety in the sheets, and self-defense."

"Well, condoms and pills are one thing. What about those "out-of-control" moments when a guy wants to get rough...all in the name of passion, eh?"

"I stick my needle in him and switch to girls for awhile."

Silence. Trey knew he couldn't compete with that choice. Didn't like to think of Shontel sampling it, but she certainly hadn't adopted it as her main thing.

"And when you go back to boys?"

"My needle's still available."

"That why you carry dual lethal weapons? Derringer and a steel hair pins? They really lethal...poisoned?"

"Yep. Mama taught me."

"So, learning' 'bout life was a lesson on how to enjoy safe sex, eh?"

"Spose' so. When my periods started...and once I heard from mama, I just blended life with sex into my future. No need to wait. Pleasure is there for the takin'."

"Pregnancy?"

"Mama showed me...the pill, shots against disease, condoms for thoughtless guys, thrills of pettin' and timin'...she told me 'bout all that."

"She tell you about saving yourself 'til you're in love?"

"She said love was a fiction, invented by insecure parents who wanted their girls out of the house before the sweet things became pregnant."

"You bought that?

"I did."

"That what you believe now? We're just having fun here?"

"I been tellin' you that since first we went out, my tall, tower of power...'member me callin' you that?"

"I do...liked it."

"Well, so did I."

"So, where are we right now in life, Shonny...can I call you that?"

"No one else has, so let me try it on for a time."

"Again, where are we?"

"We're right back where we started, Trey. I can glue myself to your body, but I can't meld my mind with your feelings. Remember my sayin' to you, 'This ain't love White Boy; it's just good sex'."

"Been tryin' to change that. I need something more. I've been wandering alone for a long, long time and I've never felt more connected to life than I am right now, Shonny. Just walking and talking with you...it fills me up. Just so you know."

"Trey...you're touchin' me in ways somehow new...makin' me want to be touched in ways you know so well, but I'm not investing myself in any timeless way with anyone. Special moments, on the other hand, they count...any soft pine in those trees up there?"

"I'll find some."

"Or up against a tree."

"I can be a stand-up guy."

"Why don't you lean against the trunk and I'll climb yours?"

"Try this."

"Well, my tall tower of power, here I am," dropping her clothes so quickly he thought they must have been zippered on. "Have it your way, my man, so long as I get what I need."

They didn't care about prying eyes or clear, blue skies. They raised a storm, threw lightning and reverberated in the thunder. And after they rested, they dressed and wandered home for another session of small talk and big releases. Just as Trey hoped. Just as Shontel wanted.

They spent time learning each other's secrets, Trey spewing his guts out about the family he hated and the professional life he loved, clearing all obstacles for the two of them to become emotionally connected. He found her listening, knowing, bonding, and he began to think they were folding into one another. Then, one morning, as though she had slipped into a new slice of time, Shontel told him she needed to be gettin' on to Chicago where she thought she could get a couple of auditions, and then to New York, for the same.

"What about us, Shonny?"

"There is always us, Trey. Just never sure when we get to live it. I'll stay in close touch, my man."

"I'll be here."

Leaving brought her a little twinge of sadness, but Chicago was a bit of a comfort, a change of scenery from New York, and a healthier atmosphere than L.A. She had appointments, meeting producers of a new film, SYNC, which would deal with the hard rains of the city and the burial plots in Lake Michigan. If she were gonna play the role written, some kind of sidewalk informant to the mob...well, she was fine with that. Truth was, she said to herself in her occasional 3:00 a.m toss and turn, she knew street walkers better than she knew the bedrooms of the rich, in small towns or big city lights.

Smiling at 30,000 feet, she revisited memories of her early years in Copa. She, a Black talent startling locals, winning regional contests for soliloquy or outstanding member of a cast. Words flowed from her in high tones or low intimacies, bringing truth, insight or explosive anger. Her face could propel simpering, aggressive, quizzical looks, imploring audiences with glances carrying to the last rows of an auditorium. She had talent, everyone said so...*and she believed it* because she knew her body, her smile and her beauty. No fool was she, and moving in and out of producer and director's offices taught her early on, and permanently, to never sell herself short. Not ever.

They descended and touched down…on time. As they taxied, she hummed. Acting filled her life, she knew, but singing moved her soul. Maybe Chicago would offer something.

She walked briskly to baggage, picked up her two cases, loaded and placed the Derringer in her handbag, and headed for Four Seasons. In the taxi, she finished off her little career review, reassuring herself that her ambitions were still valid. Film made her famous, for a moment, but she went back to Broadway regularly, concentrating on musicals, reinvigorating her sense of herself. Then, a decade into being known, her career cooled…just fell apart.

She grimaced and shifted in her seat, stared at the Chicago skyline for nearly a minute, tossing answers in her head. Agents quite calling. Scripts stopped arriving. Why? Who didn't she know?"

Who could explain it? Every actor wondered. Every actor experienced it. But it was hard for her. She didn't have to go back to Copa, but for years, in her 40s, she floated through small, off-Broadway plays, regional musicals and an occasional tv commercial. Hollywood lost track of her. She knew herself, and she was known in the show biz community, but she had yet to find the vehicle that would do what she told everyone back in Copa she would do…become a fixed star.

She paid the driver, tipped him well, registered at the desk and let the smiling bellhop take her luggage up with her. Threw her things into drawers, drew a bath, sat in it and took a deep breath…relaxed. Got out, toweled, thought about Trey, to her surprise. Ordered room service and a bottle of red wine. Ate carefully, thoughtfully, and headed to bed with the sounds of city traffic jabbing at her, and lake breezes sneaking in, whistling through a tiny leak in a window frame.

Couldn't sleep for a time, thinking about those thoughtful, challenging days with Trey, feeling those impulses he brought to their time in the bedroom. It was damn good sex. Was it anything more? What was he really after...an actress to help him create a fantasy film, or did his intensity carry with it connections she didn't want to make...had never wanted to make with any man...or woman. She was committed to her career, to herself, to all the promise that her mama saw for her, and if she were ever thinking of a long term, monogamous relationship with any person, she was not sure Trey was the one. Still, she was in no mood to reject him...or his dream...just yet. Needed to see what this film project was all about...then see how she felt about him...stay or leave. She'd done plenty of both. She slept.

Three days later, she flew to New York to see friends in Harlem, hang out in the Village and answer two casting calls, both musicals. Late afternoon, walking from Times Square to her room at the International, she tripped on a raised edge of concrete, twisted her ankle, fell and felt like she had cracked a rib, and maybe a bone in her right arm. Shaken, she went on to her apartment, applied ice and heat, but wrestled with the arm all night long. And when it wasn't hurting, her ribs were. Got up early and went into a Quick Clinic, where a nice, quiet spoken doctor took a look, examined her, took some notes, drew some blood, ran some labs and X-rays, wrapped her arm for compression stability, and asked her to return mid-afternoon. She rested in her room, returned about 4:00 pm. He walked in quietly to examine her wraps, then spoke..quietly and seriously.

"Miss, ah...," he looked at the patient information form, then at her again, and she told him, "Just call me Shontel, honey. The rest of the world does." He smiled, began again. "Miss Shontel, I am going to say a little something about your injuries and what I found in my general examination. Your arm is not broken, but I'll keep it wrapped. That will keep those strained ligaments in place...should heal fully in a week. Your ribs are a little different. Two of them are cracked, but again, not much to do but avoid stretching or aggravating them. I could wrap your chest, but I doubt you would find that comfortable, and it would not change the healing progression much at all. I'll prescribe some mild pain-killers, but nothing addicting. When the pain is gone, you'll be far from New York."

"So, I'm good to go, eh Doc?"

"There's more."

The comment set a deep twist going through her gut. She shook a little, looked at this nice, nice young man, and asked, "So, I'm not good to go. Didn't hurt anything else. S'up?"

"When I first examined you, I noticed some swelling in the lymph nodes under your arm. I drew enough blood to run a panel of tests. We pay particular attention to white blood cell counts, lymphocytes. Usually, old lymphocytes die and your body creates new ones to replace them. But sometimes, your lymphocytes don't die and your body keeps creating new ones. The oversupply crowds into your lymph nodes, causing them to swell.

"And…"

He looked at her, began to speak, paused, then said quietly, "Shontel, I am seeing lymphatic swelling and cells in your blood that suggest that you may be affected with Non-Hodgkins Lymphoma, a type of cancer. Now, I don't want you to panic about this…even if this preliminary screening proves to be accurate…NHL is quite treatable, and prognosis for a patient in such good general health as you are is quite favorable."

"You sayin' I have cancer!"

"I'm saying that you may have a certain, treatable type of cancer, and I would like to have you get a full review with this doctor whose card I will give you. Dr. Erica Long is a specialist. I work with her from time to time. She is excellent. I would like you to see her in the next few days. If you wish, I can have my office call and arrange an appointment for you. She can take you through a series of imaging and blood tests to determine what type of NHL you have and how best to treat it. Usually, especially with early discovery, the outlook is very good."

Later, Shontel would say that his words didn't induce panic, but she felt herself enter into some form of psychic retreat, a gathering of inner resources she needed to absorb his comments, to understand what they meant and what they didn't mean, and she needed to let some words come out of her mouth to make it all a reality. But all she could manage at that moment was, "Yes, please. Make the appointment."

A few minutes later, she gathered her things, tucked the information card into her purse next to the Derringer, and thanked him for his thoughtful expertise. She walked back to her room, thinking hard, closed the door, and began to rock herself on the edge of the bed, drawing what courage she could from the Doctor's words, quelling the panic rising as best she could, seeking to keep it from collapsing all of her fortified equanimity. She was not sure she could manage it. She made a decision, made it so easily it surprised her, a feeling she would have to deal with later.

She called Trey.

CHAPTER 11

TREY'S GAMBIT

Unlike politicians, the mob kept its word.
Perfect Ted

We three gathered around a small table, one of two Trey kept at arms length for quick memos and informal sketches. We knew what was looming…work on Olivia's screenplay. In it, we needed to find truth amidst the inevitable array of doubts, focus on the oddity of racist expectations, accept alternative phrasings and alter the story line until we believed in it. Temperaments would be tested, as would our resolve. We ground away at it til' early afternoon, took a break for a light meal and went at it again. I thought to myself there would be a lot more room when Trey finished building my home and the Bar Delta Ranch had a more modern flair to it. About 4 pm, his phone buzzed. He lurched to it…an unusually quick response to any interruption, I thought.

He listened a moment, then walked to another room. Must be Shontel.

A half hour passed, and he returned, sat at his desk, and looked to the ceiling, to the walls, to the floor, as though sorting through a problem…and he was. Finally, he faced the window for a few moments, a minute maybe, and I got a little antsy. I looked at Olivia. What now?

"That was Shontel."

"You don't look happy about it."

"I'm not."

"S'up?"

Trey looked at us both, seemingly confused in his own mind about what he wanted to say. Tried a few silent lip movements, then just blurted it out.

"Shontel has cancer."

Silence.

In the near distance, Two-Step Overlook rose from the surrounding terrain, presenting piney slopes, featuring a new driveway working its way through the trees to the crest where it touched the framed skeleton of my new home. I heard the nailing guns finishing the day, rattling the peace…a miniature jungle battle out there. Still waiting for information, I looked at Trey.

"That's all she said…she has cancer?"

Finally, "Well, yeah…it's Non-Hodgkins Lymphoma. Going to get treatment in New York. I don't really know what to say, Bobby. I've been working on ideas for storyboards, thinking about ways we might get some money to start a film, enjoying the feeling I get while I'm thinking about her. Everything was quiet around here…peaceful. Haven't been in such a mood in years. Just thinking of her."

"And now?"

"Well, fuck, Bobby! Everything is on the edge of a cliff. No studio wants to take a flyer on a cancer patient. If Shontel is too ill to go on with this, where are we…back spinning our fingers wondering what to do with our lives."

"That can't be all bad, Trey."

"Well, it's bad for Shontel and it's bad for me. I don't like giving up on a plan…and I want her in my life…want a future with her."

"That may come, Trey...but for now... at least she is getting treatment and they found it early I'm guessing.. You know anything about Non-Hodgkins Lymphoma, Trey?"

"Not yet...but I will soon."

"I know a little something, and I want to alert you both," I looked to Olivia, waited for her to fix her eyes on me, "to what Shontel is really telling us."

Trey looked at me, hard. "She said anything to you, Bobby?"

"Not at all, but I can help you assess your feelings, Trey. I'm good at that feeling stuff, you know."

"Go ahead."

"First of all, Non-Hodgkins Lymphoma is a serious cancer. It's treatable and it can likely be put in recession, but it is not "curable" in the sense that we use that word. It will take a toll on Shontel's energy, mental concentration and zest for life. When Delta was diagnosed with Lou Gehrig's Disease, she had been in its clutches for more than two years without suspecting a thing. First inkling she had was finding some difficulty in forming her words, and neither hard work nor therapy could remedy that."

"What's the lesson here, Bobby?" Olivia asked softly.

"If Shontel is just being diagnosed with Non-Hodgkins, we really don't know how long it has been in her body, whether it is about to overwhelm her, or merely alert her of its presence. There is something else, pretty much outside my experience with Delta."

"Spin it out, Bobby," Trey spoke softly, but he was still staring at me pretty intently.

"Well, ALS is untreatable. Stunning as it was to get the diagnosis, equally gutting was the realization that there was nothing to be done... no therapy...no drug regimen...nothing. Delta, and I, were going to have to accept and respond as best we could to her body doing less and less. Her speech would disappear...and she loved to talk...and her movements became more and more stilted."

"You've never talked about this before, Bobby."

"This seems like the moment, Trey...probably not a good time... but the right one."

"Anyway, when Delta knew what she had, she just decided to play it out. No feeding tube. Could walk in the last month of her life. Entered hospice 10 days before she died, and when I lost her, *I looked at Bobby and Olivia*, when I lost her, my strongest emotion was *relief*...not sorrow, not loss, not anger...I'd already been through those...just relief."

I had their attention. "Now, Shontel's cancer can be treated but that takes commitment, energy, perhaps radiation, but surely chemical infusions...morale-sapping clinical visits over a long period of time. You're gonna have a hard row to 'til, Trey. That's really all I have to say."

"You sayin' I should just walk away from Shontel?"

"Not at all. I'm saying that you, we, should think about walking away from this movie."

"Why? She ain't dying tomorrow. There's lots of time...maybe years and years."

"Doesn't matter, Trey. I know where your heart and mind's gonna' to be for most of the next year, and for each year after...therapy, resolution and the risk of the cancer's return...it all just drains a person."

"Well, fuck," Trey said. "Right now, we ain't got jack-shit in cash, and no line of credit anywhere, so making a movie is nothing we can start in the next few months. But I tell you, Bobby, if Shontel wants to go forward, I'm gonna do it."

"Trey...say I agree...before we can ask Shontel what she is feeling up to, we need money. Right now, we couldn't video a dog walking with our iPhone…I don't mean the dog has the phone…you know what I mean. We need a bank."

Trey stopped, looked at us …poured himself a small Jack Daniels and quietly began a saga that changed my view of Trey and my understanding of what we…Olivia, Trey, Shontel and I were going to be doing for the next couple of years. But I didn't understand how actions begat reactions and values could change as quickly as throwing on a new suit. But life is like that I guess.

CHAPTER 12

NIBBLING

The vig is the thing...remember, it's in cash.
Arlo Bullock

"Let me tell you a story," Trey began, "About a time past when I found Dallas to be quiet entry to a world I knew nothing about and how it produced a big pot of money."

I interrupted, "How does that apply to our situation, Trey?"

"Stick with me here, Bobby. There's a point. I'm gonna' describe my visit with a mob boss, Gino Marcello...start to finish...and you'll see why I'm thinking of him right now.

I think that was the first time I had ever heard Trey use the phrase, "mob boss". I looked at him and just motioned him to go on.

So, 'bout five years ago, I got a call asking me to come to Dallas to discuss a huge, urban development project Gino had bagged, and I was instantly interested. Cranked up my converted Cessna P210 and blew open that Lycoming engine 80% hustling my ass over there. Tied it down at Love Field, and soon sat in front of a massive mahogany desk edged by Gino's striking image. He wasn't exactly Texas style big...small body, mild smile, quiet personality...and a head ringed by white/grey flecked hair. Looked like a damn diplomat of some sort. Maybe a few years older than me. But as I came to see, there was steel and an afterburner inside that body. After 'howdies', he asked abruptly, 'So…you know who my daddy is?'

I did. Gino's father, Carlos Marcello, was for decades the Godfather of the New Orleans based mob, and lived long enough to groom his replacement, Dominic Ri'chard. I was edgy just thinking about their reputations

"You got any problems with that?"

"Not at all."

I pulled out my Apple laptop, a relatively new toy, toggled it on and spun it around so Marcello had a good view. Began my spiel and complimented it with an synchronized slide deck.

"What I'm thinking, Gino, is you should integrate all the development uses into one, with a common mall space, giving pedestrians freedom to move about as suits their impulses. Let me just take you through some illustrations of what it might look like."

Marcello studied the graphics on the screen a few minutes, asked to go through them again. Finally said, "So this is the housing, these are the office spaces, here's the Civic Center Auditorium, and the restaurants and shopping?" He looked awhile, a long look… murmured to himself, finally asked a question, "And what's this, *'All Worlds Center'*?"

"A catchy description of the whole property. Go one larger than *'Mall of America'*."

"My Sweet Mother!" Gino looked up, narrowed his eyes a bit and saw me for the first time. He paused, then offered me an invitation in that soft, but precise voice he carried, "The city is gonna love this, Trey, and I wanna talk about it some more. Stay over. Come out to the ranch for supper…want you to meet my family."

"Love to."

"Whoa!" I interrupted again. "You are going to spend the evening with a leading member of the mob…at his house, eating his food? Was that wise, Trey?"

"It's business, Bobby. A new side of business. Let me tell you both about the rest of the evening."

As Trey began to unpack his story, I could see him reliving it, saw the exposure to power fascinate him, light up his face…felt his treat in being embraced by the Family and realized that he has a past I know nothing about. Trey Thaxton, my friend, has friends in the mob. Doing business with the mob. Stunning. He went on with his story.

"The house was grand even by Dallas standards. Huge. Sprawling. A brick-edged, long driveway that passed through two different barriers, each automatically opening as Gino's car approached."

"Nice, Trey," I said, "I'm guessing a boss in the mob needs full control of his property, eh?"

"Precisely. Now don't interrupt me, Bobby. Let me tell this tale, and then let's talk about what it means, eh?"

"Got it. Go on."

"So," Trey went on, "Half an hour later, we settled into Gino's study."

"A little Jack?" he asked, motioning me to sit.

"Good enough."

"So what can you tell me about yourself Trey? What do you do for fun?"

"Well, I like Browning shotguns."

"Bird hunter?"

"Every fall. Texas has some great bobwhite shooting. Passion of mine. There's a private ranch, here in pine country, always filled with flutters. It's beyond belief, Gino. The dog handler is an old grey black gentleman, in full livery, on a mule-drawn kennel wagon, with three crates down both sides of the bed, each holding one of the prettiest little springers you've even seen. In my mind springers are the best to shoot over. Biggest hearts."

"Is he really letting you do all this talking, Trey?"

"He is. You're interrupting me more than he did, Bobby. Let me tell the tale."

"Sorry...go on."

So, I looked at Gino, cleared my throat.

"At lunch they picked us up in the four-seat, golf carts, took us to a meadow with linen covered tables and roses in crystal vases. The Mexican ranch girls fed us *huevos rancheros*. No alcohol. We were going out again, and the owner had a firm rule about not mixing booze and gunpowder, especially after Cheney. Damn, what a day!"

Gino was nodding, "Good for you Trey, it's healthy to have interests that inspire. Any other passions?"

"I like Martin guitars."

Marcello was strangely quiet. "Are you toying with me Trey?"

"No, what?" After another pause, Marcello rose, went to a door in the corner of the den, reached in, turned on lights and said "Look at this."

As you know, Bobby, I'm proud of my Martin collection, but I was stunned by what I saw in front of me...a room maybe 16 by 20 feet, with full height cabinets on the long walls and the end wall. The glass door cabinet split into two rows halfway to the ceiling. Inside the cabinets were more Martins than I'd ever seen at one time.

Gino explained, softly, "I grew up with the folk music thing, in Greenwich Village...had started on guitar when I was twelve. Probably the only Guinea folk-singer in the Village. It stayed with me." He made a shy little shrug, handed me one of his collection, "Play me something."

I thought for a few seconds, then starting running through the riff/chord intro to *House of the Rising Sun,* and as I began to sing, Gino Marcello teared up.

"Sofie hon, fetch Trey a 12 fret, and bring one for yourself." Sofie returned carrying two guitars, and handed me a classic D-45S. I strummed it a little, and said "I have a favorite Texas troubadour, Gino…this is one of his: *Snowin on Raton.* Sofia whispered 'Townes Van Zandt'."

"You know it?"

Sofia nodded.

"Sing it with me?"

I started the Travis picking, and went straight to the verse, Sofia came in on the chorus in a sweet high country harmony that raised the hair on my arm, at the same time playing little single note runs up the neck against my picking. I glanced at Gino and saw him slowly shaking his head.

One word review: 'Wonderful'.

Trey stopped his story-telling, looked at the two of us. Olivia just motioned with her hand for him to continue.

"I was almost overcome by the family life of this powerful, wealthy man. His wife, Anna, pretty, small featured, with raven hair that was clearly natural, was totally immersed in Gino and her family. She was enjoying me because Gino was enjoying me. More, she saw a new enthusiasm in her husband, and she sent me a glance of appreciation. The grandchildren, a boy of sixteen, Joseph, and a girl, Sofia, about eighteen, had been splendid mature young people during dinner, vibrant and entertaining. Hell of an evening."

Gino walked me to his private sedan, told the driver to take me home.

"Won't forget this night, Gino."

"Neither will I, Trey."

Trey stopped talking. Looked at us trying to assess the impact of his story and I suppose the new importance that Gino Marcello had for us. I wasn't quite sure what that might be.

Trey continued. "It's a longer story than I thought I guess, but I needed to spin it out for you both," looking at both Olivia and myself.

I still was not quite sure why we needed to hear about Martin guitars, shooting guns, and singing songs…but it was Trey, and if this is the way he wanted to tell his story, so be it.

"Again, Trey," I asked, "What does all of this heartwarming stuff about a mob guy in Dallas have to do with us sitting in Copa, worrying about Shontel?" I knew he would have an answer.

CHAPTER 13

HOLD THE BUCKET

When you're in, you're in to your chin.
Trey Thaxton

Trey looked at the two of us. "Well, it's now five years later, but I have a history with Gino, and I'm gonna go to Dallas and see if he would like to help us to get started…pre-production work, down payment on Olivia's script, laying out a film set at Bar Delta…logo, incorporation, a myriad of small things we need to be doing right away… searching out talent…things we can do while Shontel gets treatment."

I felt my stomach turn. Glanced at Olivia. She caught my eye. Neither of us liked this idea. But Trey, my friend Trey, had given me a glimpse into his life which I had never thought to explore. He had done business with the mob and was looking to do more. How dangerous was that? He didn't seem to care. He was all in, and money was money…maybe just enough to start. How much did that affect me? In and out? Buy the opportunity. Quickly pay it back, or not? I didn't like risking money and I didn't have any good feeling about dealing with Gino Marcello. Did the mob like making movies? Maybe. Did it collect debts? Always.

"When're you thinking of doing that, Trey? You sure you can just approach him on this. I've heard stories from Arlo about this Dominic

Ri'chard down in New Orleans. He says Dom runs the whole Marcello family these days. Do we need to check with him?"

"I'm thinking if Gino wants to, he can. Me, I'm gonna go straight to the guy I want the favor from. Let him clear it."

"Arlo says this Dom Ri'chard is quiet as a still night, but lethal as a coral snake...stuff he doesn't like...doesn't happen."

"Well, you tell Arlo what we're doing if you want...but so far, all I know about Arlo is that he tells good stories. I'm goin' to Dallas to see Gino."

"How soon?"

"I'm leaving in two days. Wanna come along?"

"No, thanks. I'll leave that conversations to you. I'll see what Arlo thinks about Dom Ri'chard. Trey...don't do anything that puts us in jeopardy, eh?

He just looked at me, promising nothing.

Two days later, he left for Dallas. Found himself again sitting across the big mahogany desk in front of Gino Marcello and told him the whole story...he, Shontel, and Bobby connected through time and a film production that had a "sell-by" date.

Gino sat back, quietly listening, asked a few questions about Shontel, a skepticism about her recent career, what she might...or might not...bring to the production. Was sorry to hear of her cancer, showed optimism about her recovery. Trey felt the chatter waning, saw Gino place his hands together, fingers extended, hands parting, then coming together then apart, then together again. "A thinking rhythm," he thought.

Then Gino started up again. "Trey, back in the day when my dad, Carlos, was dealing with Bobby Kennedy and that pack of fuckin' wolves in the JFK world, you know he had a hell of a tough time."

"I've heard rumors."

"They're true. One night, in the middle of the night, that fuckin'
Bobby Kennedy, sent his agents swooping into New Orleans, picked
up my dad without any judicial procedure, put him on a plane and
flew him to Guatemala. Sat him down in a jungle airport, and told
him to find his way home. Well, it was unlikely, but you know what?
He did. HE DID! And from that day forward, the family has always
owed a debt to the guys who found him."

"Never heard that before. Who were they?"

"Couple of brothers named Perfect Ted and Tricky Dick Bullock.
Both World War II vets who knew guns, gangs and gratitude. Hell,
I think they could have rescued Custer if they'd been around at the
Little Big Horn."

We both laughed at that image...and I asked, "They really have
nicknames like that?"

Gino smiled, "Yeah, seems to have been a family thing...well for a
lot of families who fled Oklahoma. Amusing. But they were serious in
their work...mostly. And Ted and Dick got my dad out of the jungle."

"Bet that helped their careers?"

"Well, yeah, though Dick moved on to California soon after. Went
legit."

"Perfect Ted didn't?"

"Not so much, but we worked well with him. He ran a small strip
joint in the Longview area, and wanted to expand. Dominic Ri'chard,
you know him, head of the family down in New Orleans now...very
young then, a fresh lieutenant, so to speak, very old now, but still in
control...anyway, he saw to it that Perfect Ted grew his business...
and kept it. I still laugh today about the way Ted reclaimed his place
in 1945 after coming back from the war."

I waited for the story, and finally, Gino gave in. "Ted walked into
his old Longview joint, told the current operator, Curly, he was back
and was taking over. Curly, says, "NO WAY"! Next day, Perfect Ted

rolled a powder grenade into the center of the place and it exploded. Blew Curly out the door. Ted, looked around and declared. 'This is my place now'...and it was."

Gino laughed loud and long. "I like people who solve problems."

"So what did Perfect Ted do then?"

"Expanded from Longview to Shreveport, then to Dallas, where he hooked up with Jack Ruby. I think Ruby was one of Dom Ri'chard's earliest political successes, long before he succeeded my dad. Anyway, Perfect Ted went on to establish a number of Gentleman Clubs in Arizona, New Mexico, Texas, and Nevada. Finally made his home in Denver. Very successful."

Trey liked the story, but where was it leading? "What's our connection here, Gino?"

"Yes...well, Perfect Ted had a son, Arlo Bullock, who really took to the business. Arlo picked up on his fathers entertainment circuit. Eventually set up a steady performing schedule for people like Fats Domino, Ella, Nat 'King' Cole, Jolting Joe Turner...dozens of black performers who needed a venue and a place to sleep and eat. Not far from their lodgings, Arlo would open a Gentleman's Club. A symbiosis of patrons, so to speak."

"That what they used to call the "Chitlin' Circuit?"

"Part of it, yep. Arlo protected his venues from the goons and racists, and he made sure local union bosses were happy. In turn, they respected the order he brought to his business. Really knew how to put a smooth plan together."

Gino paused...waited for my reaction.

"Arlo Bullock? Well, as you're describing him, Gino, I'm thinking that I've heard the name. Pretty sure my partner, Bobby Banfield, married Tricky Dick's daughter, Delta. Makes her Perfect Ted's niece...family. Delta died couple of years ago, and what with time and distance between Bobby and me, I didn't get to know her very well. But, you're saying I should reach out to Perfect Ted's son, Arlo?"

"Yes. This film plan of yours, and this money of ours, however much we invest...well I trust you, and I trust Bobby Banfield if you say so. But I don't trust movie directors and the suits who sift in and out of a movie production. I've heard some bad stories connected to making *Goodfellas* and *Godfather*. Sometimes, the reality behind the camera was worse than the fiction in front of it. So, I have a practice of attaching an associate to big money investments...to be my eyes and ears so to speak. I'd trust Arlo to do this, and if he vouches for your Bobby Banfield, well, then I have the trifecta: you, Bobby and Arlo. Our money is protected. Even Dom Ri'chard would be pleased with that arrangement."

"Well, then, Gino. Arlo is our guy. Do we need to touch base with the Dom?"

"Nah. You're good. You gonna film in Longview, eh?"

"Well, nearby. Bobby and I are building a home for him on Lake O' Pines, and I can just set up a film set nearby, use both the home and the set for filming. He has land that gives him 800 feet of frontage for outdoor shots. No movie is cheap, Gino, but I'm confident we can use this money to bring in enough to get ourselves well started."

Gino looked at me with a new expression...hard. "And of course, the vig will compound weekly, 2 points."

"I felt my balls tighten and my gut cramp a little. There it was, the pail beneath the table of food. Eat well and succeed, or vomit it into the bucket. I did not want to smell the bucket, and I needed to remember that excuses were not part of the menu. Maybe Bobby was right to be so skeptical. Well, fuck. Nothing is easy, and Shontel has an expiration date on her...a year, two, maybe five, seven. Who knew?"

"When you aiming to start?"

101

"Well, hell, Gino, soon. Now, your money won't be enough to film anything, but it is gonna' give us enough to start making calls, to line up on-site resources and to try to build credibility in the gossip community. We can promise something and techies and on-set talent will hear about it. It's preliminary work...but essential. Need to build a set and hype some chatter in producer's luncheons...prove we have a plan. In six months, your money is either gonna help us put a package together, or we will be paying you off, with smiles and thanks."

"The payoff has to be in cash, not smiles" Gino reminded me. His voice was normal again...supportive, friendly...assessing, but I knew the undertones would always be there. "Then what, Trey? You think Shontel is gonna be well enough to start? How soon?"

"Out of our control, Gino. We think her infusion treatment should be completed in six months or so...they found a tumor...but until it recedes, she's gonna be unavailable."

Gino looked at me, a little pity crossing his eyes. "Good luck with her, Trey. I like you. Whose your source on techies and casting?"

"Our screenwriter, Olivia Downey, former Dean of School of Theatre and Film at Middleton College...Bobby's old place when he was president there...she is well connected inside the film industry. She's takin' a leave of absence and gonna work with us. Has a short list of directors too. I'm thinking we'll select from that."

"Well, whoever it is...keep an eye on him...Arlo will do the same. I get edgy working with newbies."

"Will do it."

Finally, he said "how much do you need, Trey?"

"I've done some calculating, Gino. I can sell my practice for $15 million I think. And I'm comfortable trying to find some producer, a studio...big time...to fund the film."

"How much do you need, Trey?"

"Half a million, Gino. Something to give me credibility when I go into the suites of the suits...something to get us through the next few months while we start contracting with technical specialists, line up the rest of the financing."

"That's a lot of vig, Trey. Where you thinkin' of getting the whole melon?"

"Selling my firm. From that, I can repay your loan and have a good core of money left over to solicit some large investments."

"Got any sources for that?"

"Well, the traditional path is to align with a studio, maybe Columbia which is buried in Sony now, but it produced the Spider-Man franchise, made about $2.5 billion on it. Now, we're small potatoes compared to the guy swinging on a web, but if we can sell Columbia on our screenplay, we'll have the cash to make it happen.

"That's a lot of money they rolled up with Spiderman," Gino mumbled to himself, "Got to keep a closer eye on studio big-budget films."

I nodded agreement and went on.

"If that doesn't work out, we can turn to Netflix and see if they are interested. They took a shot at producing their own material a few years ago, and while that didn't work out, *House of Cards* sure did. They seem to be sucking up new programming, and we'll approach them right away...see if we can get them committed to a streaming offering."

Gino was nodding as I recited my little mini-history of Columbia that he had no doubt digested years ago. "You know, Trey, back in the day, the Marcello family had some influence there in Columbia...guy named "Donut" Dan Rosario...a little too mouthy for me, and he did sort of disappear, but still, relationships endure and the family stays active. Ask Bobby to take that up with Arlo. He might be able to tap into that old relationship, and I think Arlo did some Netflix work for another producer…a woman associated with the Ringling Circus, I think. Might be able to help. Good idea to keep her in your loop."

"We'll do it, Gino. Thanks for that."

"You keep sayin' 'we'. You got any corporate entity to work with…a production company you can park the cash in…something you can use as a front for the whole project?"

"Yep, Pinnacle Productions, gonna incorporate in Delaware, with offices in Longview and Dallas. Bobby, Olivia and I will be officers."

Silence now filled our space as Gino gently closed his eyes, and puzzled through numbers, people and projected time-lines. I knew this was his final check-point, and all I had projected for us, was, for him, a deal to be evaluated. If our hopes did not turn out to fit Gino's reality, there would be trouble…for me…for all of us. We would all be vomiting into the bucket and looking for a way out. I held my breath a bit…and watched his face.

Gino turned to me and commented, "I'm gonna let you have this at 2 points rather than my regular 3. Remember the vig starts the day after you get money and it's rolled into the principal every week, and then compounds. It is paid in cash only. In two months you will owe close to $600,000. You think you can handle that?"

"I believe so."

"You be on your way now."

I nodded and made my way out, carrying the lightness of success and the weight of obligation, murmuring to myself, "Sweet Jesus, once you're in, you're in to your chin."

CHAPTER 14

A PAUSE

A bale of hay can turn your life to manure.
Olivia Downey

I listened hard to Trey's story and tried to follow it up with some optimism.

"So, you think we have a deal, Trey? Eh? Gino bought in?"

"I think so."

"Why the doubt?

"Well, I know he'll run it by Dominic Ri'chard in New Orleans… it's a lot of bucks, and it's not in the barn yet…we'll have to wait for a call."

Olivia excused herself, began snapping her fingers together and asking on her way out, "Is this really a good thing, Trey?"

She was out of sight before he could answer. I cooked some breakfast, finishing it up as Olivia reappeared, tucking in a few strands of her hair, fresh from the shower. She sipped coffee, ate some toast, asked the question of the morning, "When's it gonna be here?"

"Soon," Trey said. "Very soon."

It came just after lunch. The phone buzzed, and Trey put it to his ear.

"This is Thaxton."

Pause.

"Go to mile marker 9…just past that there's a gang of mailboxes on the north side of 116. Turn north there and go 1.4 miles to a couple stone pillars and a sign on top that says Bar Delta Ranch. Another mile or so to the house."

A quarter of an hour later, the truck arrived and Trey went out to take delivery. He approached the rear carefully…raised the roller door, and saw three cube-like packages each about the size of an ice chest, wrapped tightly in heavy black plastic with steel binders, each on its individual pallet.

"Oh fuck….oh fuck. Gotta get this out of sight now!" He phoned Fleck Kingman, waterfront patrol at Lake O' Pines, and a handyman to have for a lot of jobs, mostly legal ones. "Where are you, Fleck? Need you here now with the front loader. Come directly to the driveway." A half-hour later, Fleck arrived, smiling as he did anytime someone else was under pressure. Trey let out a sigh, pointed to the van and simply said, "Put those black bales in the barn."

Fifteen minutes later, Trey waved Fleck goodbye, came back into the house, smiling, slapping his hands on his pants to shed alfalfa dust. I found myself frowning, rubbing the top of my head, flesh on flesh, puffing my cheeks, and Olivia began staring off into space… snapping her fingers hard…click…click…click. She blew out a long sigh and asked her question.

"So, you're saying we got the money, Trey? Sort of unbelievable and unnerving at the same time, don't you think? Is it really good news? You sure we want to get invested with the Family?"

"Well, not my first choice, Olivia,…my only option. Got to tide us over 'til I can sell my practice. Even then, we gotta find a studio to pick us up and take us to the finish. We need some start-up money now. Got anywhere else in mind?"

Bobby answered the question.

"Not yet...you know that, Trey, but damn, we gotta hook up somewhere in the next two-three months at most, or we'll be out of money, and if your practice is still on the market, we'll be running up a bill with Gino Marcello that is payable in cash only. We will never get out from under it...or should I say, we will be buried with it...eh?"

Olivia echoed the thought. "I'm a writer, Trey, not someone taking notes on how to keep borrowed cash. This is dangerous shit. I will not go dancing with mobsters, Trey. What the fuck do we do if they don't get it back, eh? What the fuck?"

Her language caught my attention. "If we lose our ass on the project, Trey, we lose our breath. What then?"

"I'm not thinking about failing, Bobby. I'm thinking about Shontel."

"Are they, Trey! Are they? Is that what Gino told you? They're worried about Shontel?"

"Look, Bobby. Gino Marcello is only thinking about washing money and having it grow in the spin-cycle. You gotta accept that, or we're done before we begin."

"So, we're gonna just sample the water...you think? Sounds to me like we're with him through the whole wash."

"We are...'til we're fluffed in the drier."

"Jesus, Trey. We could be putting our lives on tumble here."

"I think it's our only option, Bobby."

I paused. "When's Shontel gonna be ready to perform, Trey?"

"Maybe six months. She's had one treatment. Been through the tube to reduce the tumor. Three more to go and infusions, probably six about a month apart, maybe less. She should be ready to go then."

So, I thought, we have an actress undergoing radiation and chemo and nine months to get production ready for her to walk on to the set. Raw numbers tell me that the vig on the half-mill from Gino and Dominic was going to topple us in two months, maybe three. What then? Any flexibility in that time frame? I knew more than one person now taking a dirt nap had tried to bargain their way out of a deal with the mob. I'd heard stories about Dominic Ri'chard. Not good stories. "Profit or loss" suddenly had a more ominous tone about it. And yet, what other option did Trey? And what was Olivia gonna' say about all this anyway...if she wasn't in, neither was I.

"Is the clock ticking on the money, Trey?" I asked.

"It is."

"How much time can we manage before the vig becomes a calling card on our door?"

"Three months, tops. But, by then I should have some serious negotiations underway over sale of my firm. It should work."

"Pardon me, you two," Olivia interrupted. You keep throwing this word "vig" around and I've heard it used before, but I'm not really sure what it means. Why is it such a pressing issue?"

"Explain, Bobby."

"Vig is short for 'juice' or 'interest'. In the world we are entering, it is the price one pays to use money, and it is calculated and compounded on a weekly basis, and repaid in CASH. Always in cash. Can't pay the vig...you are likely to be staring at the inside of a barrel."

"Well, that helps," Olivia whispered. "Knowing that, I gotta say I'm a little more leary of the phrase, 'It could work'. I see now. <u>It has to work</u>! Right?"

"Yeah, Olivia, I hear you on this," Trey spoke softly, always a hard thing for him to do. Let me say, I'm gonna run it out to the end...not more than 3 months. By then the nut and the vig would total close to $650 thousand."

"How we gonna' cover that, Trey?"

"Guess I would say if we haven't got a studio behind us by then, I'll pay off Gino...assuming my practice has sold, and we'll go looking for another way to make Shontel a star. My pledge…3 months, and we wrap up the Gino connection. O.K.? Will that work, Olivia?"

"*But how exactly, Trey*? If your practice has not sold, the vig continues, right? We could start piling up a debt we could never repay, and it has to be paid in cash. You can't just sign your practice over to Gino Marcello. Fuck, Trey. This could be the death of us, literally."

"I'll make it work, Olivia."

"I'll hold you to that, Trey." Turning to Bobby, she asked, "How're we gonna use the money Gino's renting us?"

"We're gonna park it in Pinnacle Corp and use it to start pre-production, get some options on a film crew, techies from sound and camera. I'll see if I can find a studio interested in a risky bit of investment…but I agree with both of you…three months…fresh cash or we're done. Need something big that can underwrite the entire effort. We may be a low-budget film, but we're still talking millions."

"Any ideas from Gino?"

"Well, yeah. He mentioned something about the Marcello family once having had an interest in Columbia Studios. Thought we might do a little looking into that.

For a moment, all three of us were silent, thinking, squirming a little, Trey driven by this fixation on Shontel, Olivia driven by self-preservation, and I, driven by connection to friends, to Olivia, and, I admit it, by my desire to make Shontel happy. But I could feel my neck tightening.

Olivia looked at me, searching. "Are we still able to reconsider the loan connection to this Gino guy, Trey? Bobby?" Trey just looked at her, his eyes narrowing as he slowly shook his head, "no". He glanced at me and asked with his eyebrows. "Are you in?"

I didn't have an answer, but I felt the urgency of Olivia's concern… her growing fear…and I did have a question.

"So, Trey, that truckload was the money?"

"Yep."

"Where is it?"

"In the hay barn."

"Can we see it?'

"Sure."

We walked across the yard, looking around for no good reason, just some innate caution against being seen. Slowly entering the barn, I took a good, deep breath and thought again how freshly stored alfalfa filled the senses. Could anything smelling that good nuzzle anything bad?

Trey took a hay hook, pulled three bales off the stack, and pealed back a large, blue tarp.

"Did you count it?"

"No, I measured it, and kind of weighed it."

I started rubbing my head again. "This is our hay?"

"Yep."

"We're in the movie business, eh?"

"No," Trey spat it out. "We're partners with Shontel and the mob in the fuckin' movie business...hang on, Bobby."

Olivia turned her head to a corner of the barn, clicking her fingers...and retched.

CHAPTER 15

CHAINING THE LION

Gino had to part his hair, a warning without a sequel.
Trey Thaxton

In all the conversations I had with Arlo, one of the most dramatic was the story he told of how Perfect Ted and Tricky Dick maneuvered through the layers of protection bootleggers threw up around their product and successfully stole a huge supply of "Backwoods Hootch". Those "ridge-runners" as Ted and Dick described them, often stored their product in a large cabin and tied a mountain lion to an interior wall, with a length of chain that permitted the beast to protect the booze.

So, Arlo told me, the brothers decided they needed the product more than they feared the lion, and one night they drove to the storage depot, drilled a hole in the wall and slowly, quietly, drew the chain to the hole, reeling in the animal and snugging him up against the wood. They secured the links outside to a ground post. Once the lion was tucked up, they emptied the shed and were away by morning.

"Lot of snarlin', Ted said smiling, "But it was a perfect job,"

"It *was* tricky," Dick chimed in.

I told that story to Trey and Olivia, trying to lighten the atmosphere around the business style of our new investment partners. She didn't smile, seeing in the account another plank of truth about what we were now building. But it triggered a response from Trey who mentioned to us that Gino Marcello knew Perfect Ted.

"Gino will never forget the work that Perfect Ted and Tricky Dick accomplished finding and rescuing his father, Carlos Marcello, from his deportation into the Guatemalan jungle by Bobby Kennedy. Later on, Ted sort of rescued another member of the Bullock family, Bullet Ben. Ol' Ben began making a nuisance of himself, drinking too much, getting too 'handsy' with the women, and Gino had to 'part his hair' to correct his behavior. I had an uncomfortable feeling about that phrase, 'part his hair'. I asked Trey just what it meant...did they just kill him? He didn't laugh, so I wasn't guessing outside the range of possibility."

"No," Trey commented, "They pistol-whipped him with a .38...a warning without a sequel," he smiled, and explained, "Ted intervened to get Uncle Ben out of Dallas and put him somewhere a little safer, selling real estate in Florida. He did well there and Gino appreciated Perfect Ted's skill at solving a problem."

I was a little curious, "So, Trey, how does Gino Marcello knowing Perfect Ted connect with us and why is it in the conversation today?" Trey grew quiet...looked around a bit, shifted weight...finally spat it out, distaste lingering on every word. "Well, Gino wants someone down here to look after their investment. He trusts me, and he trusts Bobby pretty much, but as he says, there are thieves everywhere, and I only have one pair of eyes, and Bobby only one more. It is Gino's practice to always have a shadow presence on an investment this large, keeping tabs on everything, me and Bobby included. That's the truth of it."

"Well, makes sense to me. We don't want any problems with the mob...real or imagined. And we especially do not want to be in the Family; we just want to share a meal or two."

"It's a pretty big platter, Bobby."

"So, who's Gino suggesting?"

"Arlo...Arlo Bullock, Perfect Ted's son...Delta's cousin. Hell, I guess that makes him your cousin-in-law...family, eh?"

"Oh, fuck." My voice faded. I respected Arlo, and I had warmed to him as a married-in relative, a distant voice sharing stories about the "good old days". He knew everything there was to know about the entire Bullock family, and I knew he was happily married, with children, a solid citizen. But I also knew that he had become a very effective manager of a series of strip joints and booze hangouts, Gentleman's Clubs, he liked to say with a smile...operating in Shreveport, Dallas and Denver. Was that a problem for us? I was very comfortable with him...worried only that something in film production might cause him a problem, something out of the blue, and then that would be a problem for us, for me, and I might lose a new friendship, or worse. Somewhere in my guts, a spasm told me we were heading down the wrong path, and a quiver began to bubble up.

"I know Arlo. Working with him would be informative as well as a cooperative effort...But...just thinking, Trey...nodding to Olivia... that is a helluva lot of money out there in the barn. Putting it in Pinnacle Corp will keep it a lot safer than sitting in a pile of flammable alfalfa, but it may be a year before we can start filming. Every day, we're deeper in debt and we have nothing coming in. There's gotta be a better way, Trey."

"And it is?"

"Well, if Arlo's gonna be watching what we do, why not ask for help in soliciting a few film studios. He has a history in entertainment, so to speak. He may know someone connected to Vegas, or to some of the larger studios. One of 'em may be interested in a kind of Indy film. Maybe we can sell 'em on Shontel the singer/actress, not just Shontel the actress.

"That's fresh air you're letting in, Bobby," Olivia muttered, "Go on."

"The vig is impossible for us to maintain for more than 2-3 months. But if we can get a commitment from a major studio or a a temporary slot in an entertainment casino in Vegas, we could satisfy Gino right away and operate with less time-sensitive pressure. Then all things might be possible. New directions might bubble up. Might even save Trey's company."

"You give me hope," Olivia muttered.

"Well, hard to hang a half-million on that," Trey commented. "Unlikely a studio's gonna jump in and rescue an entity like us in just a few months. No, I gotta get my business sold, and I'll lose money doing it on a quick turn-around, but I swear to you both, as I swore to Shontel, I'm gonna get this done and give her what she wants most...a last kick at the cat of fame."

"But which cat is she kicking, Trey?"

He looked at me, "Whad'ya mean, Bobby?"

"Well, Shontel does a hell of a lot more than act...you know that. She can sing, dance, keep a line of patter going for an hour if she wanted to. She's an entertainer, Trey. So why do we keep trying to put her into a box...a movie?"

"Well, it started with your book. I liked it. Thought of her...we went from there."

"Where's it taking us, Trey? We're now in debt to the mob, however nice Gino Marcello seems to be, and regardless of his interest in Martin guitars...fact is, we owe him a lot of money. Half a million bucks! Olivia is puking every half hour, and I'm getting more and more nervous about sorting out studio options that could pay off Gino and fund a film. Christ, that's a lot to ask, Trey...a lot of money."

"I'll cash in my practice. Pretty much done with it anyway. That would put us right side up with Gino, and we could go looking for more money."

"Selling your practice, Trey, if that is really what you want to do, is gonna give us a nice nest egg, but no chicks. We need to find another sponsor, a major studio, and you are saying that is impossible to do it just a few months. I think you are right. Olivia thinks you are right. So maybe the idea of Shontel and a movie is the wrong way to go. Maybe Arlo could give us some useful advice about that, eh?"

Olivia practically filled the room with her exhaled breath, "My God, thank you Bobby. Seems to me we're all adrift around a big planet where gravity keeps us from getting away, and the emptiness of space draws the life out of us. I'm terrified."

"It's new to all of us, Olivia...it really is."

"Well, I believe that, Bobby! What the fuck are we doing owing half a million to a mobster! I write screenplays. I don't leverage cash, sit with dark money guys or sort through studio politics and investments. The maneuverings you talk about are probably necessary, but not if we just walk away from this whole movie thing. You tell me we're gonna spend nearly $40,000 of Gino's money right away in pre-production, making contacts, lining up some expertise and getting commitments from some placement actors." She paused, began snapping her fingers in that quiet little habit which told me to listen carefully. "I'm having a tough time seeing anything good come out of it!"

I nodded my head toward Trey and explained. "If we continue... we're gonna have to start operating in a new world...of cash, influence, rumor and spite. Making a movie is hard work, and we're still on the hunt for a good $15 million investment. Even with Shontel's starring role, we are going to need enormous resources to get attention, bring in theatre viewers, run a print and media campaign, get social sites talking and then hope for word of mouth or some other access to a large audience to make the money we have to have. If we fail, someone will be parting *our* hair…or worse. How we gonna' do that?"

Trey remained silent, and Olivia backed me again with a quiet, "That is the question."

Trey growled, "Hell, we're gonna' cross that bridge when we come to it. Shontel has an expiration date. Lymphoma can be managed for a time, but it usually wins in the end…how long…three years…five? We gotta get the movie made and then see where to go from there."

Olivia and I looked at one another, focused on an escape from the deal that Trey made with Gino Marcello. I felt less and less committed to a multi-million dollar project when we were already tossing a few hundred thousand around with no way to repay it. I was edgy, my stomach turning a bit, and Olivia still looked pale, wiping a little drool from her mouth. She began clicking her fingers.

Trey grew quiet, remembering Gino Marcello looking him in the eye, unblinking, and telling him this money was a way of laundering cash. Gino wasn't giving him an "easy—peasy" reassuring nod from a major player in the Dallas family. He was stating the terms with his eyes, and Trey knew it. Knew it from the moment he set foot back into Gino's life, 'cause his work with him a few years ago taught him how the shadow world of cash worked. No matter where it presented itself…gambling, prostitution, bootlegging, construction, garbage collection, laundry provisions, taxi service, catered food, on-line porn, dock-work…no matter where…cash was king and cash was always the laundry to be washed and the mob was in charge of the soap.

He had dipped his toe into the waterline that Gino Marcello drew for him, and he had no regrets. But he also had no way out, unless this movie were a great success. Shontel's capstone performance, to which he was committed, would die stillborn. He looked at Bobby and Olivia. "Way I figure it, we need the film or Shontel's future is dead and we might all join her ashes. The film is everything."

Well, he was right about that. The film <u>was</u> everything…the root cause of all our troubles. I felt a little singed by the dollar connection to Gino Marcello, cause we were now linked to the mob…but in a kind of arms-length relationship. I had at first thought if we didn't connect with a big studio, Gino Marcello would be resilient enough to absorb a little loss. I was wrong, and I was thinking differently now.

Clearly, we did not have months to chatter on about the fanciful idea of making a movie. We had obligations. A couple of dozen grand of Gino's money was earmarked for preliminary set work, more cash commitments to follow. Trey was selling his firm. With every passing minute, my gut rolled harder. We were on a limb, above the creek and the wind was blowing at 2 points a week.

"Look Trey, I like making the big play on big bucks as well as you do, in theory and in stories, but I don't like it in real life. I think we need to look at some alternatives here, and our first effort needs to be repaying Gino Marcello. If we can do that, we could clear our minds of money and think more clearly about how we can package Shontel. She's not goin' anywhere for six months. Let's put the movie on a back-burner. Put my book in storage. Put Olivia's screenplay in a drawer. Let's focus on first things and the first thing is to repay Gino. Chain the lion."

Trey looked at me…at Olivia, "Really. Just end it?"

"Have to, Trey. Right now, if we repay the vig and ship cash to him, right now, we'll owe nearly $550,000. Where we gonna' find that?"

"What you thinkin' Olivia?"

"The same, Trey. Get us square with Gino, and give us a few weeks to think about what else we might pursue for Shontel. Can you do that?"

Trey blew out a lot of held air, let it "whoosh", and I saw his shoulders suddenly relax, as though he had been holding this whole

project in place with his will and the strength love can give. Now...
undone.

"Well," Trey spewed the obvious, "Shontel's not doing anything special for the next six months. But if we spend all our time here, bullshitting, speculating and future-wishing, Gino is not going to get paid."

"He has to be paid!" Olivia started clicking her fingers again.

"Maybe something will work out," I commented, "I'm gonna' see what I can learn from Arlo that might help us survive."

CHAPTER 16

VEGAS

Uncle Frank taught the Bullocks all he knew, and what he knew about most was robbing banks. We don't do that anymore.
Arlo Bullock

I always had the feeling that sooner or later, my family conversations with Arlo were going to include Vegas. It was probably just my insecurity bubbling up, but as we mentally calculated the vig on that loan from Gino Marcello, we grew nervous. Just how soon could we get out of the deal, with honor and with our heads? Trey had been letting the word go out that his practice was for sale, and he had a couple of nibbles, but the offerings seemed to reflect what buyers thought was a distressed sale, which it was I guess, and the follow-ups Trey believed would surface... didn't. In two months, we would have to pony up cash for the vig, our draw on the original loans and the loan itself. Total: $600,000. Neither Olivia nor I felt our pockets were deep enough to chip in on such short notice. We just wanted out.

Trey now agreed, but where to go with our Shontel mission? I decided to strike out on my own and that meant one word, Vegas. Of course. Who would I see? I didn't know. Arlo knew a lot. I called his club in Denver, *Snowcaps*, and asked for him. He was on the line in less than 20 seconds, and I felt confident he must want to chat with me...and chat I did.

"Arlo. We three here at the Bar Delta are having a crisis of confidence in our movie-making scheme. Slipping into this arrangement with Gino Marcello gave us a boost for about a day, and then it gave us indigestion which hasn't quit. Can I talk to you some about alternatives…based on who you know and what you know?"

"Bobby, anything you need I'll try to provide. Is the vig getting' to you all?"

"The vig, the meatball and the time frame are making us ill… looking for alternative ways to promote Shontel."

"Where is she now?"

"Still in New York getting initial treatment…will probably come down here to Bar Delta after that. Trey says he'll fly her back and forth for infusions. Gotta say, mostly for your benefit, Arlo, that he is head-over-heels with her. Hard to talk about anything other than giving her a platform to find her star again."

"So, it's still the movie, eh?"

"Well, we're beginning to look at it from a strictly money angle… doesn't look promising."

"Good to think about it that way, Bobby. That's how Gino is goin' to think about…strictly money. Got your pants in a bunch?"

"It does. I told Trey and Olivia I'd look into Vegas…see what it might offer…thought you might give me some guidance there."

"You still lookin' for movie-budget money?"

"Well, yes… and no."

"Why the no?"

"Money…don't have enough…can't see getting it in time for Gino. The vig will eat us up in two-three months."

"Why you thinkin' Vegas? It had its day, but it's a lot more complicated today…not many casinos interested in washing money through films…they had their day with that…Mormons and Howard

Hughes pretty much cleaned it up. Not likely to find what you're looking for there, Bobby."

"Well, if not with the high rollers, where would I go?"

"I would think you could go directly to the studios themselves."

"Guidance?"

"I can give you a name...send an intro along...would that help?"

"Hell yes, Arlo. I'm a babe in these waters, and I don't see any basket in the rushes. Where would I start?"

"I'd start with Jumpin' Johnny Rosario, grandson of "Donut" Dan Rosario, the first Hollywood executive with direct connection to the mob. "Ol Dan loved film, actually produced pictures, and back in the day he emerged as a part of Harry Cohn's legacy with Columbia Pictures."

"I've heard of Harry Cohn, but he's just a name."

"Bobby, let me quote you what Harry Cohn said about himself...I have it here in a clipping I keep in my wallet...just a sec...yeah, here it is. Listen to this:

I may be known as a crude, loudmouth son-of-a-bitch, but I built Columbia. I started it with spit and wire and these fists. I stole, cheated, and beat people's brains out. Columbia is not just my love; it's my baby, my life. I'd die without Columbia." (1946)

"Christ, Arlo. He sounds lethal."

"Well, he knew his way around a haircut and the outside of a barrel."

"What more?"

"Well, I figured he would control the company 'til he was in the grave, and he did, 1958. And yet, however driven Harry Cohn was, no man can run a studio alone. Remember that Bobby. The face at the top always stays upright because it has a bench full of people who take orders."

"And Harry Cohn had them, eh?"

"Right to the bitter end. He could make big decisions and he could make petty ones. He could keep actors up at night worrying about their futures, and he could cull through directors until he found one that suited him. He could make or break individual talents and sleep well. He could even resurrect careers and with Dan Rosario's urging, he let Sinatra have a role in '*Eternity*'. That led to Frank's Academy Award. Were Harry Cohn to have lived a little longer, it would have pleased him to see his own likeness as a Vegas movie mogul portrayed in *Godfather*. But...again, he could not run a studio alone. For that he needed lieutenants, workmen, executives...he needed the mob."

"Arlo, did Dan Rosario actually have experience in film production or did he just hang around money and pocket a little of Harry Cohn's change? Eh?"

"Oh, he was the real deal. He flitted around Vegas as a gadfly, sometimes as a movie producer, sometimes as a conduit to washed money, sometimes as a distributor of *Tom Thumb Donuts*, his legitimate business...it kept the Feds from throwin' him out of the country. But make no mistake, Rosario was more than a pastry cook. He *produced* dough, became a voice in the film industry and a legitimate partner to Harry Cohn. He loved making his own movies and he made three of them which continue to resonate in the literature of Hollywood Mobster Flicks: *He Walked By Night, Canon City*, and *T-Men*."

"Christ," I said, "Arlo, you're telling me about the kind of guy I would have loved to know...the kind I need right now. What happened to him?"

"*Unfortunately*, Dan Rosario liked to be liked...liked his name in print...liked to be known as a film producer...liked to be associated with big names and blockbuster films. The Family does not like publicity...does not like it at all. He became a *known* member of the Marcello Family, though he worked directly with the Chicago mob, skimming money out of the casino cash flows. But being in the mob and being publicly known for it is not a formula for a long life. He finally wore out his usefulness, and one night he disappeared, to be found in 1956 in a barrel at the bottom of the ocean near Miami. Harry Cohn may have had fingerprints on the steel casement."

"Risky business out there in Vegas, Arlo," and I found myself twitching just a bit. But that was then, this is now, and I wanted Arlo to give me a name to contact. "So why mention Dan Rosario?"

"Cause his grandson, Jumpin' Johnny, is now a high-leverage guy at Columbia."

"For real?"

"He is. We talk. He delivers."

I was not exposing myself to Johnny Rosario without some kind of guidance, and an impeccable introduction by someone the mob trusted.

"Can we talk in person, Arlo."

"Always best."

He invited me to have lunch in his Gentleman's Club in Shreveport, *"Rabbits Run"* (*Bunnies Shake* was the rejoinder). Crossing the state line gave me a little thrill. Illegal transit? Nah.

Arlo had a nice club. Cajun talent, music to help Miss black-haired-long legs, wrap herself around a pole while keeping her breasts in sight and her smile luminous. I glanced, but concentrated on small talk as we sipped a couple of drinks and ordered up a gourmet burger with sweet potato fries. Chattered on a bit about politics and troubles in River City. All just little by-the-byes 'til we could get to what I needed to ask.

Finally. "Arlo, as I said earlier, Pinnacle Corp is in a vice. We've spent a little of that loan from Gino Marcello making some Hollywood producing contacts, a few visits, a pitch or two, but the vig is eating us alive. Had a big pow-wow about it couple of weeks ago and decided we needed to pay-off Gino and find another path for Shontel's revival. Trey put his firm up for sale, but no one's taking it off his hands. He does not want to tap his reserves for the bucks we need to cover loss of principle and the vig, and we figure we have about a month to find some financial way out...and maybe some support for Shontel's revival. You think Jumpin' Johnny Rosario might be interested in us? I looked him up. Connected to Columbia Studios still, right. I understand it's now under the SONY umbrella, but produces stand alone films...and they are winners: *Spider-Man, Moneyball, Girl With Dragon Tattoo*."

I stopped yammering, and was taken aback a bit, 'cause Arlo just looked at me with eyes that were either surprised at my knowledge or suspicious of it...hard to tell. But whatever, he cleaned it all up in an instant and got back on our chitter-chatter wavelength.

"Bobby...you are right, absolutely! Columbia is successful, and Sony lets it work its magic...and I do know Johnny Rosario...and he might well help you enough to satisfy Gino Marcello."

"You think...really?"

"I do. I'm gonna put you in touch with him. He hangs out at the Gibraltar Casino, more or less in charge of entertainment there. Powerful man. And over at Columbia, he has a whole wing in the studio under his control and likes taking on risky projects...either doubling up with another production company or investing fresh money of his own. He's had successes, and a few of them were great moneymakers: *Django Unchained* and *Captain Phillips* are a couple, both ending up with Academy nominations."

"I'm ready to travel, Arlo. The team is beginning to quake a bit at the pressure, although Trey is fixated on going ahead. His feelings for Shontel strangle our efforts to deal with the project on a purely professional basis, and I'm concerned about where his devotion may lead us. Put a little love-life into a business decision, and the outcome is likely to be childless. That's what I've been learning. Right?"

"Spot on, Bobby. I'll go ahead and set you up with Rosario... maybe next week. One tip. When you see him, you might mention very casually how impressed you were his grandfather convinced Harry Cohn to sign Sinatra to that role in *'From Here to Eternity'*. Maggio was it? I think so. Anyway, liken Sinatra to Shontel...both great stars with huge public appeal who had sort of fallen out of the loop. In Sinatra's case, Cohn lifted him, reluctantly, but still, he lifted him onto the top of the star list. From what I hear you saying, Shontel is ready to throw a bombshell performance onto the film audience... and Rosario loves box office and star power. He might be ready to buy in...and if he is, he won't take a month to decide about it."

We finished up with some more jibber-jabber, and I took my bunny tail all the way back to Bar Delta Ranch to report. There was joy in Mudville when I explained my hopes and my plan. Casey was at the bat, but this time, he was gonna hit a home run. That was my plan anyway.

I slept well. Olivia curled in next to me and somehow good news brought us both into an easy, loving framework, and we broke our rule about morning sex. By noon, we were properly arranged and traipsing out to the kitchen where I started coffee and mixed up my favorite breakfast: sausage n' cakes. They both came off the grill hot, and I ate to my satisfaction. We spent the rest of the day walking the acreage, dipping our feet into the lake and imagining how it might feel living here when Trey finished our home. I still had feelings for the future, not ready to just sit around and die, and Olivia felt the same, more so I think 'cause she was younger, still harboring ambition.

Two days later, Arlo called and gave me the agenda. "You fly into Vegas tomorrow; you're booked at the Four Seasons, and Johnny Rosario will come to your apartment the following morning to talk pictures and promotions. Be ready cause he doesn't jibber-jabber. He's all business."

"Thanks, Arlo. I'll do my best. Should I bring along a dozen donuts and take a bite in honor of Dunkin Dan?"

"Bobby, that is exactly what you are not to do...strictly business, eh."

"Got it." I laughed.

Satisfied, Arlo closed with, "Be good...be careful."

I could feel my heart pumping a little more firmly. I'd better be all that I could be, 'cause if I weren't, there were a lot of carrots that needed to be harvested, and I didn't really like them that much. Worse yet, I remembered, there was that vomit pail beneath Gino Marcello's table, and I didn't want to fill it, either.

Vegas...where futures are made and lives are trashed. I tossed those ideas around all the way to the little city in the big desert, and comforted myself by remembering all the money that came out of studios. Surely, some of that could come our way. Surely.

CHAPTER 17

SHE SINGS

Songs are cheap. Selling them is the rare talent. We pay for that.
Johnny Rosario

The flight was uneventful, as though to promise that everything from touch-down to a deal with Rosario would be a memorable reality. A clear, hot sky defined a cool Vegas, streets cleaned by recent thunderstorms, and even in the hard, naked rays of day, the casinos looked important. When the lights came on, they would look alluring, entrancing, unavoidable... sucking down money from every part of the world onto the tables and into the slots. Then, somewhere in the back rooms...somewhere...hands would sort the cash, stack, count and sift off a bit of it into green piles intended for corporate offices and government taxing agencies. And, despite Mormons and Howard Hughes, a little was still diverted to Families in every major city where it quietly fed two and three generations of one line or another. My "heritage" name was Marcello, and I would be heard, no doubt, but would I be persuasive to "Jumpin" John Rosario and Columbia Pictures? Snapshots would not do. I needed to sell the whole album.

He knocked the next day at twelve. High Noon? Would Cooper be at ease? I quit amusing myself and opened the door, "Mr. Rosario, a great pleasure to meet with you. Please come in. Drinks?"

"Call me Johnny...and Gin."

"Tonic, lemon twist?"

"Yes."

"I have it."

He looked at me with a bit of a skewed eye, not sure if I were sincere…judged I was and stepped softly and purposefully into the large suite. He took a chair, held out his hand for the cool, clear liquid I brought him. Looked up at me…through me…asked me to sit down across from him and began. "So, my friend Arlo Bullock, tells me you have a movie-in-waiting that will make a lot of money and win some awards: actresses, producers, directors, the whole shit show of contributors. Is that right? Whaddya got?"

"Before I unburden myself with all of that, Johnny, I would be impolite if I did not say how much I have, over the years, enjoyed film coming out of your family…from your grandfather, Dan, to your more recent offerings. I know what I pitch to you in the next few minutes will be heard…and evaluated…by a professional with a keen sense of the market and the soul of a performer, something I guess that your grandfather saw in Sinatra back in the day before "Eternity". In any case, I know whatever you decide here today will be based on the standards I want to live by…professional quality, box-office appeal, award recognition. So here you are, *I handed him my one-pager*, a flyer with a basic blurb. He took a look, lingered.

TITLE: *QUICKSILVER*

LOGLINE: Middleton College. A transgender, Black female, Dean Sara Stone plays "Who Can You Trust" with her White faculty. Cornered by a Black Chair, who identifies as White, Stone goes slip-sliding away.

SOURCE: Based upon the novel, WHY SHE WEPT, by Bobby Banfield.

Screenplay: Olivia Downey

Film is a story of transgender love, racial stress and mismanaged ambition, staring Shontel as Dean Sara Stone, Jaida Hill as Monique Baroque', and Aerial Rivers as Betsy Moran.

He looked it over…more than once. Stared off a bit and then began to question me.

"Is this a comedy or a tragedy?"

"Tragedy."

"Porn?"

"Absolutely not."

"Classroom mean or street gut dangerous?"

"Piercing."

"Gonna rile up racists?

"Hope so."

He paused.

"I know Shontel and Jaida Hill. Who the hell is Aerial Rivers?"

"We dragged her out of a chorus line. She's pretty, smart and focused…brings passion to everything she does. You haven't heard of her, but you will."

"You set this in a university. Doesn't sound violent to me. Audiences like violence. Do those professor types ever hurt anyone?"

"They do, especially when their feelings are involved. Remember that graduate student at Stanford planting a pistol, then killing his review committee when it failed him. Bet they didn't see that coming."

"That was a graduate student."

"As are all professors former graduate students. Put something in front of them that threatens their egos, their research or their travel budget and they will kill to protect themselves."

"What's this transgender, racial storyline all about. Just a queer working in a straight office, or is it some kind of crusade to change what I call the 'commonly accepted forms of conduct'."

"There is much that threatens all forms of conduct, Johnny. A Black member of the faculty, Monique Baroque' identifies as White... she is not trying to pass as White. She believes she is White. Her mission is to ridicule the whole idea of consciously structuring racial balance as a counter to discrimination in one form or another. Our lead, Dean Sara Stone, also Black, sees it differently. They clash. Our transgender Dean is screwing women and men in various places just for pleasure, something that will titillate a typical audience. They will resent it. They will want her held to standards. But they love watching nude bodies and delicate screen sex injected as part of the storyline. Finally, there are the actions of Dean Sara Stone, killing a grant donor who might change his mind...watching a young boy die without raising alarm...all to protect her sexual identify from the general public."

"There is tension here, I grant you that. Is there resolution?"

"Yes, we are holding that back even in publicity, the teaser will be, 'What's Next, Sara Stone?'"

"And what is the answer, Bobby?"

I liked that he used my first name. "It has yet to be written, Johnny. I suspect it is a secret between our screenwriter and our unnamed director."

"What all do you have invested in this?"

"Well, we have half a million plus the vig from Gino Marcello, due in about 40 days now. Trey is selling his architectural firm, and we believe it will give us enough to pay off Gino and back up your investment. That's how much he believes in this film. But there seems to be a very weak market for his business. We worry."

"What do you need?"

"Enough to pay off the loan and the vig to Gino Marcello and give us some breathing room to make another plan for Shontel."

He looked at me, then took his mind somewhere I could not go. Stared a bit past my shoulder as he seem to mentally count money, production and product. I shut my mouth. I had pitched him the best version of what we were trying to do, and if that didn't sell it then his imagination was simply not simpatico with ours.

I think maybe three minutes passed. Rosario remained absolutely still… not saying a word…just moving his head a bit this way, then the other…his eyes sometimes closed, sometimes open…counting. Then a breath, a deep one, and he stood up.

"Can't do it, Bobby. Shontel is known but no longer hot on the market. You see her as a rejuvenated star. I see her as a worn-down has been. Gonna cost some money to revive her in the 'rags and social media, and who knows what her health will be in six months…or two years. It's just not a risk I wanna take."

I had to give him some kind of response. "She is still fire on ice, maybe if we let her sing a little in the opening, maybe a theme song to emerge from time to time with her voice…something to accompany her acting. She can sell a song. Eh?"

"She sings?"

"Powerfully, reminds me of Queen Latifa with the energy and dynamic of Tina Turner. She can carve your heart out with a ballad; think Lena Horne. I'll send you a cart with some of her best recordings…be sure to listen to, *You Are My Everything* or *Uptown Girl*. She can hold an audience for an hour and no one leaves to pee."

He thought some more. I could see an idea ready to pop, but he was looking it over, caressing it…finally he sat down again and sipped his gin.

"You know, Gladys Knight has shed her Pips and is winding down at *The Rock*, the main venue at the Gibraltar Casino. Gonna be an opening there in about six months."

"What happened to the Pips?"

"Got old. Gladys never does. Maybe Shontel doesn't either."

I didn't know quite what to say to Johnny. Was he offering Shontel a residence at the Gibraltar? On what basis? And how could Shontel prepare for something like that?

"You thinkin' of inviting Shontel to settle in after Gladys?"

"Well, I'm just wonderin' whether it might work. Anything you can think of to help convince me she could draw...apart from 'sick woman entertains thousands'."

Suddenly, the weight was on me. I didn't know what Shontel would say, what Trey would say, what Olivia would say...didn't know for sure what I thought of the idea, but it was an invitation...a doorway.

"I love the idea, Johnny. We'd hire our own Musical Director and set Shontel up for one show each night, Wednesday through Sunday. No Saturday matinee. Give her plenty of time to rest in between performances."

"She can keep a schedule like that?"

"She can. As for convincing you she can deliver the goods, I have some ideas I would like to run by my partners. But a residence here fits her health issues and gives us something we can work toward. My problem still remains though. Gino Marcello, the loan and the vig."

"If we have a deal, Bobby, we'll take an option on her and pay off Gino Marcello. That's pocket change out here. You sell the residence to Shontel and your partners. Let her prove to me she can draw and perform, and let's talk again in about three-four months."

"Lots to do, but she'll be ready. We have a deal, Johnny."

He got up, shook my hand, smiled warmly and left directly...I held my breath 'till the door closed.

My God! We had a way out!

I began to breathe more normally...then began screaming so loudly it brought banging and a loud, "Shut the Fuck Up!" from next door.

I did.

CHAPTER 18

CHITLIN' CIRCUIT

For Black entertainers, findin' a place to eat and
sleep was harder than makin' a Top Ten hit.
Arlo

I remember Arlo talking about how first his dad, Perfect Ted, and then he himself had mixed ownership of his strip joints with managing Black touring professionals working what was called the Chitlin' Circuit. An unfamiliar term to me, but I learned the phrase was a description of *chitlins* (pig entrails stuffed with good stuff) and a post-WW II need for Black performers to find food and bedding safe from racist assaults while they performed the blues, jazz, and rock n' roll that mixed audiences loved to hear.

With a little web searching, I found that the circuit still had venues, not so hidden these days, but still catering to many unrecognized Black musical artists who filtered through Saturday nights until they could emerge into national prominence. Back in the '70s, Perfect Ted rubbed elbows with Cab Calloway, Ray Charles, James Brown, Fats Domino...and the idea of locating professional musicians next to Gentleman's Clubs became so widespread that one could find them linked in more than a hundred venues, from Houston to Bay St. Louis or up the river to Memphis and Lexington. In time they included

Chicago clubs, the Royal Peacock in Atlanta and at the top, New York's Cotton Club.

As word circulated, the Black stars of tomorrow showed up and toured: B.B. King, Sam Cooke, Ike and Tina Turner, and Otis Redding broke through to White audiences, but they stood on the shoulders of another hundred who made their way through the Circuit at a time when chitlin's was the main meal. Perfect Ted and later, Arlo, protected these venues. It was just good business.

That's what I wanted for Shontel...small or smallish audiences who would let our lady sing the blues, 'cause when it came to push, she could skitter your feet in jazz, vibrate your gut with pop, sway your hips with swing, but best of all, she could move your soul. Acting may have been her history but when Shontel sang the blues, she left her audience stirred and shaken.

If we could get her bookings in the next couple of months, get her out on the circuit in three, we might be able to show Johnny Rosario that she could build a crowd, draw a tear or a shout and give him a reason to commit to her for a residency at *The Rock*. The time line was close, but short strings were part of our daily accounting. Shontel recovering had to segue into Shontel performing, and that was the message I took back to her, Trey and Olivia.

We started the conversation over early morning coffee, all of us having had a good night's sleep and relieved to have shed a half-million dollar debt to the mob.

Trey began. "So, Bobby, the short version is that Johnny Rosario is willing to give us time to try Shontel in some of the blues clubs around the country, and if she knocks 'em over, he'll likely see that as a reason to bring her to Vegas, to follow Gladys Knight in *The Rock* at the Gibraltar Casino. Right?"

"Exactly." I turned.

"Whadya think, Shontel?"

"Bobby, I feel what you're trying to do here, but it's been a long time since I sent an audience home singin' the blues. No doubt I can do it. But can I do it in this recovery phase. Every infusion sets me to bed for a few days, and I gotta have 'em for at least another three months. Touring is hard. Will treatment leave me energy for performance, or for film tryouts...the kind I know I can give if I'm healthy?"

"I believe in you, Shontel, and I believe you can do this. Forget about film. We'll concentrate on structured stage performances that can give you time to rest and let you keep gaining strength. I will personally guarantee that the venues will be welcoming, supportive, hospitable and sold out. I'll invite Johnny Rosario to come out and have a look about the time we get to *The Hundred Man Hall* in Bay St. Louis. Hell, that's right across the border from New Orleans. Pete Fountain hung out for years there...drew crowds from around the country. Win that audience and you'll have Rosario licking his chops at the idea of you taking a residence with him. Sweep the Cotton Club and he'll be offering you more money than you can count."

"What kind of money is that White boy?"

"Elton John got paid $500,000 for each performance...each one. You'll get less, maybe half to start. Prove yourself and the enchilada gets larger."

Shontel's eyes widened and she looked at me with both skepticism and hope. "You fuckin' with me, Bobby. That kind of money doesn't show up in stage entertainment. Never."

"Shontel, I am amazed myself, but think about it. Elton John sells millions of records, has performed on stages around the world drawing audiences that had to be housed in stadiums. Why would he want to hang out in Vegas for six months for a couple of million bucks? Eh? He wouldn't. Make it worth his time...half a million per show... per show, and he could not say no. Similar salary structure for Celine Dion, about $350 thousand a show.

"How can it be worth it? I don't see it."

"The audiences are drawn as a bee to the queen. They will pay big bucks to sit in the audience. The Casino earns about $650,000 per show from ticket sales, and the tables and roulette wheels take in after-show dollars. Find the right performer, and it's a gold mine waiting to be flushed.

Glanced at Trey, who nodded. "Everything I have heard tells me Bobby is right."

Shontel took Olivia's hand and said, "What you think, girl?"

"Do it, Shontel. Let's just do it."

She paused. Took a breath. Then she spat our orders. "O.K. Trey, build me a studio and hire a musical director and I'll start creating my songbook here at Bar Delta. Bobby, book the venues. Olivia, you are now my White shadow. Rent me some portable mikes and speakers, tape recorders for now...and serve as my audience...keep me honest."

And just like that, we all had assignments and energy to match. A deal's a deal, and ours with Johnny Rosario was looking a lot better than the one Trey struck with Gino Marcello. All the talk and fear of vig and compound interest disappeared, and we focused on putting Shontel out there on the road to Vegas.

Within two weeks, Trey had hired a team to build a recording studio in the home he was creating for me, and a month later Olivia and Shontel moved into it and continued working through songs, tempos and styles. Trey had also identified a Musical Director he wanted to interview. William Cunningham. The dude had guided successful albums for Terry Guard, Gloria Rains and Fats. We all chittered like high school kids, feeling the power of embarking on a musical journey. Olivia practically glowed, relieved she had an experienced musical director coming to guide the rehearsals. Her own work with Shontel now shifted into that of Personal Assistant and Chief Booster.

Another week, and Trey asked Cunningham to visit Bar Delta and sign contracts. I can't say I took to the guy. He arrived at Longview National on his private jet, walked out of it with bleached hair pulled back into a pony tail, a cigarette burning in his left hand as he wiped his right across his brow. Apricot colored trousers touched sandals anchoring him to the tarmac, and a blousy, blue shirt, with three-quarter sleeves, reshaped itself with every stride. He sported a tan, of course, but his face was deeply wrinkled with lines from both tobacco and sun, and he sported a light scarf around his throat. He walked toward us, and I realized how tiny, so very tiny he was. All that loose clothing must have been designed to puff up his stature, but as he approached I could see he stood 5 feet 2 inches, maybe, and I doubted he weighed more than 110 pounds.

He postured as though a giant, staring at a horizon far beyond, so as not to become contaminated with small town greetings. His dark brown eyes evaded ours, sending out his message, "I'm here. Make me feel I'm special." We tried. Olivia gave him a "Darling" and a light kiss on each cheek. I tried a manly handshake, which he evaded and grunted, "You must be Bobby." Trey just looked him over and nodded, as did Shontel.

Every move Cunningham made set us a little on edge, but his studio success could not be denied, and Shontel needed expertise breathing compelling notes into her musical choices and delivery. While he strolled about the property, getting the feel for creative impulses, we four huddled briefly and assured ourselves we had the right guy. But in that very moment, he went on to say something that put pellets in our pants. "The most important part of a Musical Director's craft," he said, gradually raising his tone to emphasize his pronouncements, "is his mental focus, his determination to bring his vision to the soundboard, to control the studio and guide an artist to do her best work. When we have that, we are ready for Shontel to go on the road, win a following and release her album. If she wants to follow that up with a residence in Vegas, so much the better."

"I want you all to understand that in pursuing that goal, I pay no attention, no attention at all...to money. You three may be producers, but I am the musical director. I am not a budget manager. Find someone who is. I do not clip studio time for dollars, and I will not, I repeat, I WILL NOT tolerate guidance from afar or impromptu comments during recording. In that spirit, and I am sure with your understanding, you must realize that I work alone, with soundboard and engineers beside me. That's it. Once I begin, you three...he looked at Trey, Olivia and me...will not be allowed into the studio. Is that understood?"

I looked at Trey, glanced at Olivia, my eyes speaking loudly, "What the fuck?" She shook her head slightly, counseling patience.

Trey tried to work around what we came to call the Cunningham Conundrum. "Well, say now, Cunny, you know that Shontel, is suffering from Non-Hodgkin Lymphoma, gets regular infusions and really needs to be supported while recording...physically and sometimes emotionally. When we start setting up rehearsals, we really can't let her just be there alone. I'm sure you understand that."

"If you need to get another Director?"

"We do not. She is our artist. Accommodation must be made," and Trey's voice began to rise, that baritone encompassing some of the focus and power which he could produce at a moment's notice. Cunny responded with not a whisper of accommodation in his voice, but an alternative plan.

"Well, I'm sensitive to Shontel, he glanced at her...that's her name, right...I'm aware of her health issues. But, I've been through all of this before. I know what works for me, Mr. Trey. Let's try it my way for a week or so, and see what you think about the product. We can always work around little difficulties. I can keep you informed on general progress and let you have a listen to each track we make. I am game to do it. Do you see yourself clear on this, Mr. Trey?"

I wanted to inject a "fuck no" to Cunny, but Trey had set a margin. If he wanted to bend it, his call. Olivia just stared. Shontel was listening, assessing. For her, it was old news for directors and moneymen to argue about takes, energy, phrasing and tone. She could see both sides, and she could see the third side, how pissed off Trey was getting with our director. And yet, we needed to bring Shontel into a successful studio environment.

So, we just waited for her to comment. She seemed a little intrigued, paused, spoke quietly to us. "Never saw a White boy yet who didn't want to be in control...I'll manage him 'til he thinks he's managing me. If the product is good, I'll keep him working. Everyone all right with that? Trey?"

"We'll try it." He turned to Cunningham.

"I'm good, Cunny. Get your ass back on your plane, gather your thoughts and I'll build your studio. You'll have your privacy so long as the product tells me your doing something worth keeping. Do you see *yourself* clear on this Cunny?"

Our Musical Director sniffed, something in the air...maybe the cattle...then glanced beyond all of our faces, again that look into the distance. Was he posturing or creating? Finally, he simply said, "Yes. When you're ready, I'll be here, assuming you have signed my contract, my first paycheck clears and there is an extra thousand cash in my pocket each week." So, now he was impugning our financial integrity and demanding under the table payoffs. I jumped at the former and Trey the latter. As Cunny turned to leave, Trey growled, "Fuck you, Cunny." No rejoinder. He climbed into his limo, waved a little short armed goodbye and sank out of sight. A short drive back to Longview and...wheels up!

We all took a breath, passed another look at one another and assessed the dynamic. Clearly, we were not off to a good start with our Musical Director. At the same time, we had reserved options to accommodate Shontel should she need additional support.

"Shontel, when you going back to New York?"

"Another couple of weeks, Bobby. Then, I'm gonna stay here and have Trey fly me over to Dallas for follow up appointments. Thought we would move into part of the new place, Bobby. It should be far enough along to make that work, and soon as the new studio is ready, we'll call Cunny back and start recording. He's a petulant prick, I know. But maybe he can help me get where I want to be."

Well, "Mr. Trey" was hanging on and Olivia was comfortable. Shontel was ready to record and would bring her unique energy into the mix. The only person I had to check on now was Arlo. I needed to book some venues on the ol' Chitlin Circuit.

I texted him, our usual way of initiating conversation, and sure enough, within a few minutes, we were talking our way to our next meeting, skirting the real subject, but affirming that I saw him working on our new project as part of our ongoing relationship.

We met in Dallas, at a long-standing successful Gentleman's Club he owned, "*Cattle Prod*". They gave you a small, plastic, branding iron when you sat down...sort of a souvenir. A customer could gently wave it when he wanted service of one type or another. I set it aside, and focused on the new plan for Shontel.

"Arlo, you've mentioned your dad had a lot of experience in creating and profiting from the ol' Chitlin Circuit. You got any family stories that can help us plug into some of these venues in short order. Shontel's keen to start. Johnny Rosario wants to see proof of his pudding, and we three are all committed to seeing her perform for Vegas audiences.

"You bet, Bobby," Arlo commented, "I've been through projects like this before. My dad told a lot of stories about what life was like with the Chitlin' performers...no housing, no café's, no real security for Black talent. He used the circuit to link into his own Gentleman's Clubs in several cities, and once he got involved, he did a lot of good in a lot of places not connected with his strip joints."

"Don't often hear about that side of the Family's commitment to civil rights."

"Well, dollars speak, Bobby. You know that. Hadn't been for his work and that of the mob I doubt the Chitlin' Circuit would have been successful. He and his friends simply insisted that venues supporting Black performers be protected. I don't think I have to tell you, Bobby, that when the mob offers protection, there is security."

Arlo reached into his coat pocket. "I have a photo of my dad with five other guys from the New Orleans Family. It always brings a smile to my face. There's Perfect Ted, sitting with mobsters on the right, killers on the left and money men across the table. Everyone is well dressed, and he looks completely relaxed, casually enjoying a meal with them. These guys could reach into all parts of the country, one Family to another, and the Chitlin Circuit encompassed dozens of cities, including big venues in Chicago, St. Louis, New York, New Orleans...and I could go on and on.

Even as Arlo described the group, I took note of his comment that they were all nicely groomed. Maybe I'd start wearing a nice shirt, a tie, sport coat...modest, long, and subtly powerful...maybe change to a suit for evening events...a suit...I laughed to myself.

"They worked well together," Arlo went on, describing each one of them, "and that guy," pointing to the fellow on Perfect Ted's left, Mario Fellacci, "Mario...he was a piece of work, someone they had to watch, cause the first time anything went wrong with any business in any city, they would hone in on the local boss, and Mario's first response, always, was 'Well, let's just kill the guy'."

I took a breath. Arlo smiled, "And people wonder where Jack Ruby got his marching orders about Lee Harvey Oswald. Keepin' order on the Chitlin Circuit was child's play for the Family."

"Arlo, just between you and me...stories of hit men and smiling assassins do not give me comfort. I have new goals. I don't care anymore about movies, production costs and mass advertising. I care about music...promotion, a couple of hits and a residence in Vegas."

He laughed. "Hey. Not to worry, Bobby. Now that Gino's square with you, my only concern is to watch over the unions, and mine don't operate in Nevada."

"Well, someone is minding the store out there, I am sure, and by the time we arrive I hope we carry enough clout to blend right in with them. For now, I need some influence in booking these Circuit sites for Shontel. We figured she can be out on the road in a couple months to prove she is up to her standards. She'll need rest between engagements. Can you help me with that?"

"I can. How many you want to book?"

I gave him my minimum list. "Build on this, Arlo. You know the territory."

1. Royal Peacock, Atlanta
2. 100 Men Hall, Bay St. Louis
3. Cotton Club, Harlem
4. Club Handy, Memphis

"I can do that, Bobby. Give me a couple of weeks."

"Let's go eat some good food. I'm buying."

Saying that felt good...like I was in control. Maybe I was.

CHAPTER 19

LA VIEN ROSE

Music revives the soul. Shontel plants it permanently in your heart.
Melody Maynard, <u>Vegas Notes</u>

The timeline now fixed, we had three months to get Shontel into rehearsals and on the road, a month to see if she could deliver the goods and another month to go into rehearsals at *The Rock* and make Vegas take notice. Trey completed the new studio in the home he was building for me, and we invited Cunny back to the Bar Delta so he could begin working with Shontel.

He showed up in much the same mode as he left: arrogant, dismissive and authoritarian. Shontel kept looking at him with reservations, but until they were in the studio, she couldn't comment. "I want him to get me to where I want to be," she said, "And I may have to listen to a lot of hard words to get there. So, let's see how it goes."

Cunny seemed to soften a bit as we sat down and signed contracts stating terms of recording controls, and his share of Shontel's success on the road and in *The Rock*. We had some cash to keep him happy, and the following day, he and Shontel, along with 5 session musicians Cunny had hired, drifted into the studio and began working through its sound, microphone placement and atmosphere, adding a few pots and plants, a bit of furniture and some easy sipping tables. He wanted Shontel relaxed, as did we, and she was. As Cunny described it,

Shontel and the session players would record six tracks demonstrating her range and then he would bring in accent players on their own schedules to record backup arrangements and fill transitions.

It all seemed to be very professional, and for three days, Shontel sat down for supper, smiling, in a good mood, optimistic, and we three breathed a sigh of relief, keen to hear some production results, but respectful of Cunny's insistence on privacy 'til he was ready for a review.

The first number he showed us, a cover of Diana Ross', *Touch Me in the Morning,* sent us all a-shivering, Shontel smiling with that electricity she carried, asking, "What you think 'bout that White boys?"

Trey just looked at me and I returned the amazement as Olivia whispered, "Oh my God, the girl can sing."

"I gotta say," Shontel smiled again, "This Cunny guy may be an asshole to the world, but he knows his way in the studio. He asks more of me than I think I've got, and I dig a little to find it...and there it is. We're gonna win this game, Trey."

And just as we began to relax about Cunny, things disintegrated. Three days after hearing the opening track, Cunny turned to an up-tempo recording, *Wild Women Don't Have the Blues,* a cover of Ida Cox's hit. The title says everything about how Shontel planned to approach it. If there were any aspect of her personality that lurched and exploded with a tease, it was the wild in her. Reminded one of Janis Joplin, only Shontel could sing.

She walked into the studio with her hair loose and her stickpins wedged tight up against her scalp, dressed in a halter top and shorts high enough to walk a deep river. She wanted up-tempo, intense horns and a driving rhythm from drums that would transport her into the lyric, and she loved the phrase, *"I never was known to treat one man right.*" "That's the truth in the song," she commented to Trey, "and that's what I'm singin', the truth."

But that wasn't Cunny's view. He shut down the rhythm section, brought in some violins and a lonely flute and told Shontel he thought it should be a ballad, something to win over a romantic audience. She disagreed. They argued for a bit. He raised his voice. She screamed "Go Fuck Yourself, Cunny," and within 15 minutes the entire session had broken down. Cunny sent the musicians home. Shontel stormed out of the studio. Cunny fashioned his cigarette holder and took a smoking break, waiting for Shontel to return.

Trey, Olivia and I were sitting at the table enjoying a light beer and a pastrami sandwich when she stormed in with her whirlwind of anger and dumped rain all over us. "That Cunny is a one-trick pony," she began. "I ain't gonna sing 'bout wild women chasin' their doin's and presentin' it as a ballad. Not gonna do it! He can do it my way, or get the hell out of here."

Now, this was the Shontel we all knew. Argumentative, demanding of standards and interpretation, not to be contradicted, and ready to crush anyone and anything that she felt would destroy her creative efforts. Right now, Cunny was on the wrong side of her line. For how long we wondered? Trey's cell buzzed. He looked, glanced at us to indicate it was Cunny, and took the call. We listened from our end. "Hi Cunny," Trey began, and then went silent for almost 20 seconds. Then, "Well, sure, I can see how you feel that way, but she's the artist isn't she? It's her work that gonna be out there. She's gotta believe in it."

Silence. Then from Trey, "Uh-huh. Yep, I understand, and all I can say, Cunny, is you gotta do what you gotta do. Have a good flight."

Trey touched off the phone, looked at us, "Cunny's leaving. Says Shontel is unmanageable. Says we broke the contract. Says he may sue. Says he's done with the whole pack of us."

Shontel rolled her eyes, "That honkey thinks he knows something about music and interpretation...all he knows is what rolls up in his pants...and leaks down his leg. He's gone. I'm good. I know what I want...just need someone in the control room to work with my engineer to produce my style, tempo and range of intensity."

"Want us to go lookin' again, Shontel," Trey asked?

"No Trey. I just want you to take over the job. I have confidence in you. You know something about guitars, song and mood, and I know you're in my corner. We aren't producing classic country here, but you know the blues, the romance of a lyric and musical edges. Asking an artist to think about what she...meaning me...wants and how she might go about it one way or the other is something you do well. Yep, Trey. I think you're my man."

And back into the studio they went, no one missing Cunny, though I had some uneasiness about his comments regarding "breaking a contract" but hell, if he was gone, that was good and in the next month, all four of us rejoiced at what Shontel was recording. Trey let us listen to each track in early lay-down and again in polished form, and we loved it.

Take *Wild Women*...for example. Shontel brought near chaos to the lyric, driving her own sense of fractured boundaries into every word, letting her abandonment of protocols fill the phrasing and letting the listener rejoice in her well-founded opinion that safe was silly...wild fulfilling.

If one wanted hot and anguished, she covered Bonnie Rait's, *"I Can't Make You Love Me,"* a breathless whisper telling the listener exactly how heartache was contorting her soul. Cunny would have liked it.

And so it went. She took Etta James', *At Last* and made it a sigh of relief so large you could park your memory in it. She gave *Love Me Like a Man,* an image of her battering the bed with as much gusto as any guy might try to match. She followed it with the aching Chris Connor's, *Try a Little Tenderness,* which seemed contradictory to Shontel's usual tone, but which she turned into a weeping plea.

Everything was going well in the studio. Trey puffed with both pride and affection at the way he and Shontel worked together. She seemed to soar with creative freedom, and he found himself more absorbed in every move she made. Even her recovery was going well and flights over to Dallas became more of a vacation for the two of them. I had never seen Trey brighter.

Arlo kept in contact with me and together we identified eight, old Chitlin Circuit venues we booked for Shontel. My plan was to get her out there, twice a week, in historic settings, and let her voice and personality do the rest. I'd invite Johnny Rosario to view her in Bay St. Louis, and again at the Cotton Club when she wrapped her tour. The only thing missing from her song set was a number embracing her audience with the love she felt for them. I finally asked Shontel to try *La Vien Rose*, and it quickly became as much a signature song for her as it had been for Edith Piaf.

When we began her *A Month With Your Woman* tour, we were a well-oiled team. Trey carried his title of musical director with grace... and power. Olivia served as Shontel's personal caretaker, keeping quick notes and quips for use on stage. I hovered in the background, looking over venues, making sure we collected our cash payments for each performance and subtly plying my connection with Arlo and the mob as a feature of my business dealings. I felt a little prideful that I kept every manager in line and cash flowing in the direction intended...our pockets.

I began to dress differently. Gone were the open-throat dress shirts, soft sweaters, with arm patches, and the jaunty slacks that marked a university academic. I was in a serious business now, working with serious friends and pulling down serious money. I bought an array of ties, and used them, smoothed my pants and lengthened their cuffs. I began wearing a sports coat daytime and a suit, one of several, in the evening. Gave thought to the idea of buying a hat, wide-brimmed and smooth. If I were operating with Arlo, I needed to look good and businesslike. What the hell...we were successful promotors looking for cash, lining up friends and marking enemies. Success? We planned to find it in Vegas...stardom for Shontel, satisfaction for Trey, security for Olivia, and power for me. Birds of a feather...we ruled the roost.

CHAPTER 20

CROSSIN' OVER

A guy's gotta do what a guy's gotta do.
Bobby Banfield

I saw us on the move now, free and clear, locked and loaded, ready to make a big reveal in *The Rock*. Recordings complete? Check. Pre-release promos airing? Check. Reviews of Shontel's work? Check.

When I asked Johnny Rosario to visit the tour in Bay St. Louis, he showed up and couldn't help breaking into a smile. Said nothing by way of further commitment, but his body language told me we were in the pocket. When Shontel hit the Cotton Club, the lines outside for each of her performances wound down around the dark corners and into the alleys. People were so keen to spend their money, we had to screen for green, and run a cash only campaign so scalpers could not soak up space on the internet and gouge Shontel's fans. After Rosario watched her sing, he showed up backstage with the contract we had been hoping, praying, wishing for.

It may not have been Elton John or Celine Dion's paycheck, but a quarter-mill *per performance* wasn't sniffin' money…and it folded nicely into everyone's back account, and there were additional contracts for the three of us: Trey, Musical Director, Olivia, Personal Assistant; me, Financial Manager. I found myself enjoying the atmosphere, the ease with which Johnny Rosario slipped us into Vegas suites, Vegas conversations and Vegas stardom. Shontel's face was outside on the big sign...her name always in caps...her stardom becoming more assured every week, and there were miles and miles to go. Hard to think of a downside, but then it showed up.

It came in the form of our old nemesis, William Cunningham, our one time, one session, musical director. We heard from him only twice, once when Shontel's reviews for the Chitlin Tour soared. He wrote me an email reminding me that we had a contract with him. I ignored him. Then, when the Vegas residence became a sensation, he emailed me again, stating briefly that his contract with us was still valid, and he was expecting 10% of Shontel's revenues. He was even kind enough to tell me where to send the money: 1204539204, Routing Number: 824500278. Weston Savings, Burbank, Ca."

I suppose a year earlier, I would have gone running to Denver to corner Arlo and ask for advice. But that was then, and this was now, and I had grown a lot putting finances together for our Chitlin Tour and our Vegas residence. I had listened carefully to the lessons Arlo offered, digested some of the strategies of Tricky Dick and Perfect Ted, and felt superbly equipped, "reconciled and fully accrued".

I could handle this, and I would. My first assessment was to ask myself the question, "Was that contract valid?" I brought it out of the files and read it closely, three times. It gave Cunningham payment for the Vegas residence, or any other musical work Shontel might do for the rest of her life. Christ, it was a Colonel Tom Parker kind of contract, and I had signed it. Blew it!

But in the world I now travelled, validity was not enough. Respect was more important. Cash more important yet. There was no way we were going to compensate this little bedbug for undermining our album, antagonizing Shontel, trying to pocket cash, smuggling payments, and stealing. My new set of values taught that a bad contract, was washable. Question for me was, what to do: negotiate or regurgitate.

No court of law was going to find in our favor and that meant "Cunny" won and we paid. Strategy number two was to explore the likelihood that he could be distracted or discouraged from continuing to claim payment or any kind of creative control. And that took me back to lessons I inherited from Perfect Ted through his son, Arlo. As I went down the options to persuade "Cunny" peacefully, factoring in what I knew of his personality, his bizarre behavior, his thievery, I became convinced nothing in the world of law or compromise was going to solve my problem, which was to solve his problem.

So, without leaping into any maze of morality I found myself migrating away from values about truth, justice and the American way, and leaning more strongly on less talk, more action and a permanent settlement. If there were anything working with Arlo had taught me, it was that sometimes hard decisions turned out to be easy ones, because the alternative was simply unacceptable.

I gave Cunny one chance, offering him a one-time settlement of $350,000. He promptly rejected it, and I conceded the point to him, but said I would act only after meeting with him at Bar Delta. He agreed. Three days later, after sending Trey, Shontel and Olivia off to buy a new sofa, along with groceries, booze and toilet paper, I settled into the living room of my new home, placed a frame chair with a high back on a very large, heavy, decorative plastic sheet and waited.

His taxi showed up. I let him in and pointed him to the chair. He was still a tiny, tiny man, still sporting a rat grin, still setting me on edge just being in my sight. The plastic crinkled a bit with his steps, but he settled, his head resting against the cushioned backing on the chair. He looked around a bit, focused on me and said, "Got the money?"

"Right here," I said, "A drawer full of bucks and it's all for you."

His eyes brightened as he realized he was going to get what he had coming. He would indeed. I went around to my desk, opened its central drawer, took out my Barenta-M983, with silencer, and shot him right in the forehead. No talk, no mess, no fuss. Well a little mess on the chair behind his head, but I had a plan for that. I took a moment to savor his deflation. Felt good. I thought to myself, "nice work" 'cause his eyes got real big right there at the end.

Within the next 30 minutes, I had the chair converted into kindling piled outside awaiting an evening campfire. I wrapped "Cunny" in the plastic sheet, sealed him into an ionized barrel with pre-drilled holes, and put him into the fishing skiff. Easier than I thought to tuck his 110 pounds into a curl. Harder than I thought to roll him into Lake O' Pines, but Fleck Kingman assisted, as he helped me with so many small business decisions. We got it done. The metal settled, blurbs of bubbles saluting me, as it sank into the mud. It might rust out in say, 50 years. Only downside was I cracked a bone in my leg, hauling the barrel into the boat and whacked it again helping Fleck roll Cunny into the waters. Healed slowly. Cane needed, but I thought, a walking stick might look fashionable in a dangerous sort of way.

Cunny was gone. We had our money, and Shontel had a residence at the Rock in Vegas. My standing with Arlo and his shadowy friends was becoming more substantive, and I was emerging as a member of a new family. Danger there, but still, today, all was good.

Crossin' over turned out to be easy.

CHAPTER 21

CELEBRATION

Helluva night. Never forget it.
Bobby Banfield

I picked my steps carefully, moving slowly along the sidewalk, gently maneuvering my walking stick as though I were born with it. It irritated me that I needed it, but a third leg made every walk a pleasure and every step a certainty. I looked around a bit, pointed to a few friends I remembered, whispered into Olivia's ear. She laughed, reached up to stroke my chin, and renewed her gaze at the crowd. She searched small groups of classmates and one time friends with whom I seemed so comfortable, and wondered how many stories were floating out there...waiting to be told and retold. I had my own target.

My eyes swept again, and I saw her. Shontel...Black skin shining, dressed in a flowing Dashiki featuring panels of black/gold/white. She had her hair pulled into a bun with that dagger hair pin in place, chatting and setting a tone of fun amidst a small group of women.

Three arms length from her, Trey...towered over a group of men, most of them a bit bent. Still, I thought, he would have had a head above them even in their younger years. Had to admit, he looked great...lean and powerful. If nothing else, the mob connection had improved our style of dress, and I puffed a bit in my tux, not at all shy about its blood-red bow tie. Bold, but elegantly understated. Was that it? Who was I kidding? I was showing off...and loving it.

Well, I thought, it was a big night for us all. High school graduates coming back for a Class Reunion, the 40th, featuring Shontel Williams the local girl who was now a first-name only star in Vegas. In her first residence following Gladys Knight, she had electrified Vegas, and Johnny Rosario waved a three year contract at her, offering an annual four month residency in *The Rock*. He set Shontel's <u>nightly</u> performance rate at $350,000, and made separate provisions for the three of us: Musical Direction (Trey), Personal Assistant (Olivia) and Business Manager, (me). All I had to do was keep the money flowing into the right accounts...ours.

Was there a downside? Yes, and it showed itself slowly, not in year one, but in year three, when Shontel became more and more weary, a kind of endemic fatigue that she fought through when on stage, but one which sent her into rest strategies to get prepared for the next performance. We all knew what that was all about...the Non-Hodgkins Lymphoma...but her doctors had cleared her to work, simply noting that while the disease was in remission, it would take its toll. Surgery and radiation, infusions and meds had done their work. She was repaired, but still, she was not well.

We all observed the changes. We all ignored them, feeding off her stardom, banking our money, letting Shontel soak up the applause and adulation. Early on, she did go back into the recording studio, and produced a dazzling array of passionate, energized and romantic tracks, singing the blues amidst flavors of pop and jazz. Multi-talented she was, and her album reflected her interpretative powers in ways that beguiled listeners. Streaming services bought in. CDs sold out but she resisted making another album, avoiding over-exposure, she said. I thought it was more about exhaustion.

Still, she was wired to bring her persona back to her hometown, now absorbed into Longview. To puff up local pride, Trey spent a week going around town, meeting people, letting the name "Shontel" play out in chats and whispers about her "private life", hometown pride and Vegas celebrity. I didn't feel at all left out. I was now Pinnacle Corp's "money man" both because I had learned the ways of the Family from Arlo and because I liked knowing where our investments were buried, "buried" being the right word, I smiled, thinking of Cunny. And now, I was well connected in New Orleans, Chicago, Vegas and Dallas. It was a large world, I thought, but invisible unless you knew where to look.

Despite my ins and outs, I knew the effort it would take to get national attention focused on a small town event…a high school class reunion in Copa, Texas of all places. It took wheeling and dealing with Vegas and a little muscle in high places. The idea of a September event appealed to no one in the film, tv, streaming or video business. But there was the Family business, and I had learned from Arlo how to cultivate it. I got a five-minute New Orleans audience with Dominic Ri'chard, now 94, but still making sense and laying down Family rules. I explained, "Can't see celebrating a small-town girl's achievement without a home-town jamboree, so to speak." Dom agreed, and I knew we were gonna have our way. Told Arlo and he laughed, "He still makes good decisions. Perfect Ted would feel the same…get in the way of Shontel and someone might die." Someone did die, but I wasn't commenting on that.

None of the network people wanted to take Arlo (and now me) lightly. They knew who and what we represented, and Shontel was a raging hit. Indeed, we signed a deal with FOXFIT for a documentary covering her emergence from wanna-be Broadway to might-be Hollywood to now-is a Vegas star from Copa, Texas.

We three high school friends had hit the Trifecta and Olivia made four. I smiled, mentally reconstructing our journey together, beginning with Trey's tie in with Gino Marcello giving us a starting stake; my contacts with Delta's cousin, Arlo; meeting with Jumpin' Johnny Rosario; the Chitlin' Circuit. All connected and for flavor add Olivia, who kept multi-schedules, recorded money flows and regularly renewed my zest, humor and focus for living a good life.

Shontel led us all down the stretch, despite her illness, and re-created herself with a buzz that kept her on the cover of a handful of national publications, network morning shows and gossip columnists. She visited Colbert, whom she stunned with dress and wit, and Kimmel, whom she brought to tears laughing at her descriptions of William Cunningham. She beat Fallon in beer-cups and her banter with Seth Myers, candid, filthy and funny, sent her name trending and more offers flooding my office. Her single recording of *"Will You Be Mine"* topped the charts for six weeks, and she had a standing invitation to get back in the studio whenever she felt like it. And she would...when she felt like it.

Shontel glanced over the shoulder of her chatting partner, saw me, smiled, disengaged and walked over, nodded gracefully to Olivia. I greeted her with a light kiss, held her at arms length and just absorbed her (she was thinner now, less luminous), laughed as she shook her finger at me. "MMMMM-mmm," she hummed that two note song of approval, and said, "Bobby Banfield. You look dressed for an angel's funeral!"

I smiled. "We're all feelin' it tonight, Shontel. Olivia's tellin' tales 'bout time in the studio, how you moved her to tears with your song while you laughed at her breakdown."

"Lies, Bobby, lies," she laughed and faked a move into her purse where I knew the Derringer was hiding.

"I surrender, girl. Residence at *The Rock*. That's what its all about, and we got it made, eh? You, performing with the energy of a woman 15 years younger than your birthday and Vegas as in love with you as it was with Elvis, Celine and Elton."

"Oh, Bobby, you know me. With my voice, I can look and act any age…you remember?"

"I do. Keeps me in my place, but it doesn't keep my thoughts from drifting into places they shouldn't go."

"Bobby Banfield! You are still a bad, bad boy," and she laughed even as she looked at Olivia with that special warmth that made every comment about me both informative and innocent. Shontel. Her voice floated that special low resonance of joy that kept me awake a lot of nights back in the old days. Had to admit, she still warmed me.

As though instructed by silent message, the three of us turned toward a rumbling growl and looked straight into the face of an approaching Trey. He towered above us, full of smiles, arms open wide, welcoming us into his haven of fame. He roared again, his baritone searching for edges, but smoothed with his deep look into Shontel's eyes. The two had spent the last couple of weeks, sorting things in Trey's new home, the one he built for me, the one he and Shontel now owned.

Well, Olivia likes my old place and visiting memories of Delta had become more of a comfort than a loss. The acreage was there, cut alfalfa still smelled sweet and the silence cloaked Olivia and me with gentle thoughts and new imaginings for a couple touching old age. A cane for me, a reminder of what can happen when you tilt a barrel and forget to dance out of the way. Family business.

A few swollen joints for Olivia. Not bad. Survivable. Life still enjoyable, and last night, we four just hung out in my place, sorting through memories and drama, satisfying newly acquired tastes for wine and fame. We remembered many things, none of them far from our experiences with Shontel, the mob and the suits. She laughed and laughed when she retold her story of how she sent Cunny packing. (I didn't share my Cunny story.) And now here we were, flooded with memories of our Black superstar, she glowing, taking up celebrity space, her career in full throttle, again. Just the way she wanted it and just the way we worked to make it.

Her health…well…getting by. It was a little unsettling to see how she could burn an audience into flames, greet them with style and smiles, and less than an hour later, suddenly need to sit, to rest. It was as though she were on some kind of schedule where her body allowed her a certain freedom then reigned her in…and the freedom hour was shrinking. Shontel worried me, but she was on a roll and Trey puffed with commitment, still waiting for her to say, "I love you", those words she believed to be reserved for someone, sometime, maybe.

On the Copa Gold Carpet, we shared a few more private murmurs, turned and walked into the huge tent. I maneuvered my cane subtly, carefully, and guided by a traveling spotlight amidst a standing ovation, we took our seats…front row, centered…adjoining seats empty. The crowd grew quiet, and from behind a drape at the back of the stage, one displaying Shontel in gigantic proportions, Trey's live musical overture emerged from a whisper to an embrace, and the audience relaxed. The tent was stuffed, six hundred Texans scattered in reserved seats, rubbing elbows with smiling members of the Family and a couple of dozen Hollywood stars hiding in the audience. The entertainment press had tagged us, "The Kids From Vegas".

From her seat, Shontel bent over and whispered something into Trey's ear. I couldn't quite hear it, but I knew he'd tell me later. She then rose gracefully and ascended the stairs as though on air. Walked to center stage, looked left, right and into the heart of the darkness out there, cued the band, and began, *"I Will Always Love You"*.

Then she went into the identical set we first took on the road. Touching, raucous, embracing, loving, she reached into herself and let the audience savor a performance unlike anything in Copa's past. Maybe it was Shontel's best set ever. She was home and she was a star.

Well over an hour later, mixing in her song list with a half dozen impulse numbers, she slowly emerged from a prolonged silence, and began the vocal, *"Hold me close and hold me fast"* she asked her audience, and it reverberated with the love she offered. With the last note, the spotlight went black, as did the stage. Tent lights slowly illuminated, timed to fully glow in ten seconds and hold.

A long silence froze everyone in the dark as they digested what Shontel had managed to give them…60 minutes not lost in time but fixed in their memories…an event which framed its own existence. And then it began…a murmur of sound rising to an ovation, wrapping the audience around all four of us. Took several minutes for the applause and shouts to begin to fade, swell again, and then slowly ebb. We three turned, cheered the voices cheering us, and as Shontel swayed and smiled, we gently waved the crowd out the door.

Once the tent emptied, we three joined her up on stage, wandering, taking little mental snapshots of the times we had spent together searching for a night like this. Five years, one reunion to another; Vegas making a Musical Director out of Trey; Arlo showing me the ways of the Family; Olivia attending Shontel, elevated far beyond the concerns of a Dean of Theatre and Film. And our star who was…we could see…strung out by illness, but who now claimed an entirely new persona…a vulnerable one, edged with the gutsy contradictions of both feigned humility and the courageous marshaling of her talent.

As though to celebrate her transition, Shontel clasped her hands together, and began gently whispering her song, *"Hold me close and hold me tight…"* pointing to her imaginary audience, raising her arms, slowly marking the arc before her, till her voice plaintively whispered, *"La Vien Rose"*, settling into the ennui which seemed to capture her so often lately.

Looking weary now, she asked Trey to take her home. "Been a hell of a good night, boy-toy. Time to recline." He called the limo up to curbside, and they enjoyed the quiet of the short trip to their new place facing the lake. He took note of the shoreline, the moon reflecting a luminous, defined path over the water, from pebbles to the heavens. They paused, went inside, settling on the sofa as Trey undid his tie, dropped his jacket and slipped off his suspenders. A deep sigh. There was a future out there, and he was gonna' find it with her.

Shontel rested beside him, a little breathless, but still fueled by the energy of the evening. She took special pleasure in the echos of the audience, adding to those pages she held in her mind…the playhouses she filled, the cities she conquered, the producers she still spoke to and the ones she had silently destroyed. A quirk, she thought, that the Derringer in her purse had been pointed, but never fired. And now, in the shadows, she could feel Trey, looking on, protecting, nourishing, reconciling her strength as fame followed her every move.

It all felt so locked in place. Skittish thoughts began flirting through her emotions, surfacing in her mind: mama…schoolgirls… theatre…faceless men and women, Black and White…New York… learning a craft…sorting an image…Broadway, Vegas, Hollywood. She began releasing her breath, to relax in the comfort of the evening, humming aloud that lyric: *Hold me close and hold me fast.*

Hearing it, Trey did.

He turned to her. "Say it to me again, Shontel, just the way you said it in the theatre tonight." She gathered a breath, looked him in the eye, and whispered, "Trey, I love you." He heard it, felt it fill his soul even as he heard her breath release. He reached to caress her face. She turned it away, and he cupped her chin, her cheek, only to find it softening. "Shontel? Shontel?"

"SHONTEL!"

CPSIA information can be obtained
at www.ICGtesting.com
Printed in the USA
BVHW040209261022
650302BV00001B/1